NELL & THE NETHERBEAST

Andrews McMeel Publishing
a division of Andrews McMeel Universal
1130 Walnut Street, Kansas City, Missouri 64106

www.andrewsmcmeel.com

23 24 25 26 27 SDB 10 9 8 7 6 5 4 3 2 1

ISBN Paperback: 978-1-5248-8244-0
ISBN Hardback: 978-1-5248-8472-7

Library of Congress Control Number: 2022949596

Editor: Hannah Dussold
Art Director/Designer: Tiffany Meairs
Production Editor: Brianna Westervelt
Production Manager: Julie Skalla

Made by:
RR Donnelley (Guangdong) Printing Solutions Company Ltd.
Address and location of manufacturer:
No. 2, Minzhu Road, Daning, Humen Town,
Dongguan City, Guangdong Province, China 523930
1st Printing – 03/20/2023

NELL & THE NETHERBEAST

ADI RULE

Illustrations by Ash Szymanik

Andrews McMeel
PUBLISHING®

For Collette,
who is even more delightful than the Netherbeast
and even more terrible

Contents

From a Stone Tablet
Unearthed Outside Cairo, c. 2500 BCE
[Translated from Original Hieroglyphs]

It comes from the desert
It wears the night and the darkness
Eyes like the sun
It brings chaos
King Sneferu, the golden falcon, hereby decrees
He shall build for it
a pyramid

From an Illuminated Manuscript
Scribbled in the Margin of a Heavily
Damaged Page
*[Discovered in the Catacombs of a French
Monastery, 14th Century]*

I sawe a blacke catte yn the wyndowe
suche a piteous look yn yts yelow ie
perchance yt craves mete
I shal share myne supper

the catte hathe urinated here
suche a wycked smelle

*[Here the text becomes indecipherable, obscured
by what appears to be a small paw print in ink.]*

From a Field Notebook
[Found in a Leather Satchel Next to a Charred
Pair of Shoes
Andes, Chile, 1835]

Spotted it again tonight! It is pretending to be a
cat *(Felis catus)*.

Specifically, a domestic shorthair with black fur
and yellow eyes. It very likely lives in this glade.
Will set up an observation post in the shrubbery
and await the chance to sedate the creature with
blow darts.

Can't wait to get it back to the lab and dissect its
brain.

[Present Day]

The Netherbeast enjoyed being a cat.

Most of the time, it got almost everything right. It had midnight black fur and yellow eyes like exploding suns. Its tail was long and bendy. It had two ears, left and right. The left one had a triangular nick taken out of it at the edge like a tough cat would have.

The Netherbeast had broken-glass claws that poked out from the tops and bottoms of its paws, and sometimes halfway up its legs. (Its claws were its favorite parts.)

It had a fuzzy, squishy tummy. But if anyone tried to rub it—CHOMP! The Netherbeast had developed a taste for fingers. (Not that many people ever tried to pet the Netherbeast. It smelled like rancid garbage and looked like it had been hit by a bus.)

The Netherbeast enjoyed sleeping behind the dumpster of the Cape Green Mini-Mart. It enjoyed moonlight, fighting with other cats, and dragging the guts of small creatures across the pavement so it could roll around in the mess. The Netherbeast was not at all interested in having its own cat bed, canned tuna, or a warm lap.

That is, until it met Nell.

CHAPTER ONE

BLUE RASPBERRY SLUSHIE

Nell Stoker was not looking forward to summer in Deer Valley helping Aunt Jerry at her country inn. Last time Nell went to Deer Valley, she came home with a tick the size of a grape lodged in her armpit. Armpit-Grape Tick. That was what Nell thought of Deer Valley.

But *Lulu* was going, so Nell was getting dragged along. That was just the latest annoying thing about her big sister.

On Friday, instead of packing, Nell wandered grumpily downtown to the Cape Green Mini-Mart. They probably didn't have mini-marts in Deer Valley, or if they did, it was probably just giant ticks behind the counters.

Nell pushed the door open and lurched into line. Three kids from her class were ahead of her. Nell hung back, pretending to examine the wrinkled hot dogs in the heated glass case with the little rollers on the bottom.

"Oh, hey, Nell!" One of the kids turned around. He raced bikes, she remembered. Motocross. Last fall he broke an arm. There had been signatures all over the cast because he was popular.

Nell searched her brain for something to say. Nothing came. She searched some more. Still nothing. She cleared her throat even though it didn't need clearing, making a weird honking noise.

"You haven't got rabies from the strays down at the shelter, have you?" asked the kid with the Sprout Real Estate cap.

"Not yet," said the kid with the mustard stain on her tank top.

The three of them laughed.

"We're just messing with you," Motocross said.

Nell knew that, but it still hurt. Not a lot. Like when a dog nips you because it's scared, but the nip grazes the bone.

As her classmates bubbled out of the mini-mart, Nell approached the counter. "A blue raspberry slushie, please."

"What?" dripped the teenager wearing a name tag with the name rubbed off.

"A blue raspberry slushie," Nell said again, louder. People always said *what* to her.

Nell took the fat plastic cup off the counter and shuffled out the door into the dirty alley next to the mini-mart. It smelled like the trap in the kitchen sink if you let the gunk in it fester for a few days. She slid down the wall and sat on the slimy pavement to sip her slushie.

She hadn't even said goodbye to the shelter animals. Most of the ones she knew would probably have been adopted by the time she got back from Deer Valley. She was abandoning them. Why didn't anybody understand that?

Character-building, Mom had said. Nell knew what that meant. Nell and Lulu's parents were always trying to force them together in the hopes that some of Lulu's Lulu-ness would rub off on her sister. Lulu was compact and quick, and she knew what to say to classmates in line at the mini-mart. "What are your plans for the summer? Any big races coming up?" Lulu would think of it and she'd say it, easy as flicking a flea from a comb. Nell, on the other hand, was half a foot taller than her sister, even though Lulu was four years older. Nell was not compact. Not quick. When April Springfield, the meanest girl in school, called Nell a moose behind her back but loud enough for Nell to hear, Nell thought, *She's not wrong.* It didn't matter. Nell's parents could make her go to Deer Valley, but they could *not* turn her into her sister.

Bzzzzzz. Nell's phone vibrated in the pocket of her red jeans. She pulled it out. The text ID said SHANA, the director of the Cape Green Companion Animal Shelter.

Hey, Nell, I know you're headed out today, but I've got a very upset Mrs. Baskerville on the phone about a fancy rat?

Here we go again, Nell thought. It was true that Nell had a knack for finding lost animals. So far this spring, she had reunited three dogs, two cats, and a cockatiel with their worried people. Shana always checked in when a new mystery came up, as though Nell had some kind of magic power.

Really, Nell was just observant. She listened and watched. It's easy to do when nobody talks to you anyway.

She quickly thumbed a response.

mr squeakers is not missing
He likes to hide in the couch. Mrs B always
forgets.

She's very insistent that he's been kidnapped.
Ratnapped? Apparently he's been gone all
morning. She's talking about going to the police.

She is always going to the police.

Tell her to check between the cushions

. . .
Are you telling her

. . .

She found him!!!
Great job!!!!!!!!

Nell stared at the heaps of exclamation points, but she didn't feel like an exclamation point. She felt like an ellipsis, the dot-dot-dot that means you're not sure what comes next . . .

She leaned back against the alley wall and slurped a sip of blue raspberry. She was going to miss Shana's exclamation points. It would be a long summer with no mysteries to solve, nobody to hang out with except Lulu and Aunt Jerry, and no animals to care for. Nell didn't have a pet of her own—the one thing she wanted more than anything in the world. Mom and Barb said *no*.

"Mrow?"

A fluttery, growly sound came from the shadows at the corner of the alleyway. Nell looked up. A filthy black cat with glowing yellow eyes was headed straight toward her. For some reason, it made the hairs on the backs of her arms stand straight up.

CHAPTER TWO
THE NETHERBEAST

Nell took a long sip of slush and peered at the cat in the alley. It was dirty and ragged—clearly homeless. It stared at Nell from the other side of a green puddle. Its eyes were weirdly shimmery. It was almost like there was something else inside them—something larger, darker, and deeper, filling the alley, peering out.

"Mrow, meow?" The cat hopped over the puddle and began to purr. Then it rolled onto its back and batted its little paws, revealing its fluffy black tummy.

After all her time volunteering at the shelter, Nell could tell the difference between stray cats, escaped cats, abandoned cats, and feral cats. But this creature didn't seem like any of those.

In fact, it didn't seem like any cat Nell had ever seen.

The black feline arched its back and wiggled its tum some more.

"No tummy rubs for you," Nell said. "I'm pretty sure you'd eat my fingers." She squinted. "There's blood at the corners of your mouth."

"*Vreee!*" the cat shrieked, opening its mouth wide to reveal long, red teeth. The shriek rang in Nell's ears like a giant mosquito. Two chickadees fell out of the sky in alarm and lay stunned with their feet in the air.

This is a terrible cat, Nell thought. Then she wondered, *What would it be like to adopt it?* It wouldn't make her more popular, that was for sure. But for a moment, she imagined . . .

"Who wants to read aloud next?" the teacher says, looking pointedly at the back of the classroom, where Nell hides her face. "Nell? Nell

Stoker? How about you? Would you like to read aloud? Would you like to read this passage from The Red Badge of Courage *aloud in your stupid moose voice for the class?" Nell tips up the lid of a picnic basket hidden under her desk . . .*

A fearsome black cat springs forth!
Yowling like a banshee!
Striking icy fear into the hearts of everyone in Reading Block B!

Nell cracked a smile in the direction of the strange feline. "I'd like a cat like you." She sighed. "But it's not gonna happen. *No pets,"* she added in her best Mom voice. *"They're too messy."* Even though Lulu was just about as messy as anyone could be, and Nell's parents let *her* live in the house.

The two chickadees came to and sped away, back into the sky. The black cat lashed its tail in annoyance. "Boww!"

"Oh," Nell said. "You're *hungry*." She poured a bit of slush out onto the pavement. "Want some of this?"

The cat puffed up and gave her an indignant look. But it sniffed the slush, then licked. Its space-explosion eyes widened in delight.

"Mow!"

Nell couldn't help a laugh. "And it turns your tongue blue, too." She stuck hers out for the cat to inspect.

The black cat stuck out its own blue-stained tongue. The tongue was short at first, but it stretched and *stretched* and curled . . .

. . . until it was two feet long. Its owner took a good look at it.

"Roww!" the cat growled with approval.

WHAT?

Nell looked this way and that—had anyone else seen the cat with the *two-foot tongue?*

There was nobody around. She raised her eyebrows. What would Mom and Barb say about *that?*

Nell took a big breath. "I hate to tell you this," she said, "but it's pretty obvious you're not what you seem to be."

The cat blinked. It sat primly on its haunches and fluffed. Its eyes got bigger and cuter. Every single razor-claw *shwooped* back under the surface of its skin. "Mew?"

"Look, you can say 'mew' all you want. I don't buy it." Nell shot the animal a meaningful look. "I can *tell*. You might be able to fool other people, but not me. I'm a cat person. And you are not really a cat."

The not-a-cat hissed. A rumble of thunder vibrated the pavement. The sky turned black.

Nell's arms sprouted goosebumps. She jumped to her feet. A growly, bloodstained, stretchy-tongued beast that could turn a sunny afternoon into midnight? It was amazing!

But, yeah—she needed to get out of this alley *now*.

"I, uh, I have to go," she said, backing away slowly. "I have a date with a tick."

The cat stared at the blue deliciousness in Nell's hand. It wanted more. And by the way its red teeth flashed, Nell was pretty sure it was planning on a couple of fingers for dessert, too.

"Rrrrrrrrr," the cat rumbled like the deep ocean. Ribbons of electricity started frizzing through its fur. It took a step toward

Nell, its broken-glass claws scratching the pavement.

Only now it was as big as a border collie.

Nell froze. "Look, you don't have to get all . . . all . . ." Her voice stuck in her throat. The slush trembled in her cup.

Nell gulped. "You want more slush?" she asked.

The cat continued to advance, growling and scraping. Now it was as big as a sheep and still ballooning. It was angry and fluffy, its front paw—now the size of a saucer—nearly touching Nell's sneaker, its rotten breath warming her chin, crimson teeth chomping.

Something clicked deep in Nell's bones. She straightened her shoulders and narrowed her eyes. "No!" she said in a stern voice, pointing right at the huge, black nose. "That is *not* how we get treats!"

The cat paused.

It blinked.

Then, slowly, it sucked away its glass claws and razor teeth, defluffed, and shrank back to cat size. The sky returned to summer blue. The cat stared at Nell curiously.

"Okay, then," she murmured. "That's better." Her voice faded and her shoulders slumped again. "You may have some more."

She dumped a bit of icy blue onto the pavement. The now-completely-normal-looking cat gave a little chirp of delight and lapped it up with a cat-sized pink tongue.

Nell nodded in satisfaction. She wasn't sure where all that confidence had come from, but it had worked. "Nice kitty."

The cat tilted its head at her.

Nell almost patted it. Almost. "I guess I'll see you around, you—Netherbeast." *Netherbeast.*

Where did that name come from? She didn't know, but it felt right. She smiled a crooked smile. The Netherbeast was strange and scary and didn't quite fit into the world. She liked it.

The Netherbeast's yellow eyes followed Nell as she left the alley; she could feel them on her. Her arms were still goosebumpy. She didn't look back at the creature in the shadows. If she had, she would have seen it start following her on padded paws. She would have seen, in unmistakable cat language, the Netherbeast's sleek, relaxed fur, slim pupils, and forward, upright ears.

The Netherbeast adored her.

✦ ✦ ✦

CHAPTER THREE

LULU

The Netherbeast followed Nell all the way out of the alley and onto the sidewalk. She noticed him a half a block down from the mini-mart as he clattered over a grate.

"I can't play anymore," Nell said. "Lulu's probably flipping her shoes right now wondering where I am."

"Mow?" The Netherbeast cocked a greasy ear and kept trotting after her.

Nell shook her head. "Nuh-uh. No way. We're going to Aunt Jerry's today, and I can't just go packing random creatures of the dark realms into my suitcase next to my socks."

"Mew mew?" the Netherbeast warbled, shimmying his butt. "Meeeeeew?"

"I *can't*," Nell said. "I'm sorry. You have a very nice dumpster back there. Go enjoy it."

Honk! Honnnnnnk! Honk-honk-honk! A car laid on the horn. The black cat fled into a storm drain. Nell kept ambling down the sidewalk, sucking on her slushie.

"Get in, buttface!" bawled the voice of this year's Cape Green High Student Council President. "Hey! Nell Stoker!"

Nell took one final gulp of blue raspberry. It gave her a brain freeze.

Honk! The car pulled to a stop next to her. It was long and yellow, like something out of an old movie.

Nell's sister, Lulu, had gotten a great deal on it. "Just wait until you have to get parts for it," Barb had said. "They'll cost an arm and a leg, if you can even find them." But Lulu didn't listen. Not listening was one of her superpowers.

Now Lulu was leaning out of the driver's window, wearing enormous sunglasses and an irritated frown. *Of course* she had piled all her stuff next to her in the front seat, leaving only the back seat for Nell.

"Get in this car!" Lulu whined. "What are you even doing? I want to get to Deer Valley before September!"

Nell's older sister had always been annoying. But at least Lulu used to be annoying in an interesting way, like when she smushed a banana on Nell's head at the beach or applied rainbow eyeshadow to Nell's face while she slept. Now, Lulu wore boring eyeshadow and only used bananas as a source of potassium.

"I don't want to get to Deer Valley at all," Nell said, tossing her cup into a recycle bin.

Lulu made a sound like a rhinoceros who couldn't get the lid off a jar. "You are *not* going to mess this up. I need this summer job. Living at college is expensive—did you forget?"

As if Nell could forget. It was all Lulu talked about. She couldn't wait to fly out of Cape Green High and flap away.

Never mind that all of Nell's plans had gotten messed up by this mandatory vacation in the land of ticks. Mom and Barb didn't care two cents about the Cape Green Companion Animal Shelter. They didn't care that Nell was finally old enough to be a Junior Volunteer, only to be hauled away for the whole summer. Nope, all they cared about was *character building* and *sister bonding*.

Nell would rather have bonded face-first with the sidewalk.

Lulu revved the car's engine and smacked the door. "Get in, you big, horrible stick insect." She adjusted her huge sunglasses. "Didn't even get me a slushie."

"Get your own," Nell said, reaching for the back door handle. The car jerked forward a couple feet. Nell almost fell over into the road.

Lulu's face was innocent. "What's the matter? Get in, will you?"

Nell reached for the handle again, and again the car lurched forward. "Come *on,* Lulu!"

"Sheesh, just open the door," Lulu said. Nell could have strangled her with her own stupid-looking jeweled ribbon necklace. But she finally grabbed the handle and slid into the back seat. Lulu's old car roared out into traffic.

"I packed for you. You're welcome," Lulu said.

"Thanks," Nell said. She closed her eyes and exhaled. It calmed her down. "Did you make sure to bring all my ugliest clothes?"

Lulu laughed. "Of course."

Nell laughed, too. It felt kind of good. She levered her sneakers off and propped her feet up on the back of the front seats, which were actually a single vinyl bench. "How long will it take to get to Aunt Jerry's?"

"*So* long." Lulu sighed, dragging out the *sooooo.* "If I didn't need the money, I could've lived the rest of my life without setting foot in Rose Cottage again. What an albatross."

"A what?"

Nell didn't have to see Lulu's eyes to know she was rolling them.

"An albatross," Lulu repeated. "It's like a big, stupid, expensive thing you can't do anything with. A huge pain in the butt that you're stuck with."

"Oh," Nell said. "I know all about *those*."

Lulu laughed at that instead of getting mad. "Hey, at least you're getting out of Cape Green for two months."

Nell frowned. "Sure. Just when I *finally* get to be a Junior Volunteer at the shelter."

"Yeah, about that." Lulu's expression in the rearview mirror was hidden by her sunglasses. She looked like a huge bug. "You're . . . not quite a Junior Volunteer. Yet." She cleared her throat. "Surprise!"

Nell's breath got faster, even though her voice felt smaller. "But—my birthday was last week!"

Lulu's giant bug eyes tilted into the mirror for a second. "Shana told Mom and Barb you weren't ready."

"*What?*" Nell had been waiting and *waiting* for her twelfth birthday so she could officially become a Junior Volunteer at the Cape Green Companion Animal Shelter. She went there every day after school, swept the floors, did the laundry, played with the "kid-approved" animals, and Observed. So much Observing. Nell wanted to *do*. She *knew* she could do so much more to help. Plus, a responsible, important Junior Volunteer would *certainly* be ready for her very own pet. Not even Mom and Barb could argue with that.

Nell had worked so hard. How could Shana still see her as just a Little Helper?

Lulu sighed. She sounded just like Mom, which was annoying. "You're *not* ready, Nell. You have to learn how to get along with people, not just animals."

Unlike Nell, Lulu had a lot of friends. They were all annoying like her.

Nell's sister kept talking. "Shana said helping out at the B&B this summer is the perfect opportunity to prove you're grown-up enough to be a Junior Volunteer. Easy, right? Especially since *I'll* be there, too."

Sure. Never mind the fact that Nell and Lulu couldn't even bake cookies together without one of them throwing a fit and dumping flour all over the other.

"And just imagine," Lulu said in a snotty voice, "a whole summer without your constant aroma of bleach and urine!"

Nell crossed her arms. So Shana was sending her away, too? What about all the animals Nell had helped? So much for all those *Good job!!!!!* texts. Those weren't exclamation points—they were *lies*.

And how did Lulu know so much about it? Was everyone having secret meetings about Nell?

"Here." Lulu tossed a plastic box into the back seat. It was full of old cassette tapes. Nell's sister had rigged up a tape player to the car's radio. She was pretty good at gadget-y stuff like that, Nell had to admit. Of course, none of Lulu's friends knew about that side of her. Lulu had figured out long ago that building strange contraptions made you about as popular as spending all your free time scooping cat litter.

"You can pick the first tape, albatross junior," Lulu said.

Nell pouted for a few seconds. But there was no point. She started to dig through the faded collection of 1980s hits. Then she felt something fuzzy brush against her arm. There, on the seat next to her, was the Netherbeast.

CHAPTER FOUR

THE DEAL

"You brought a *cat?*"

Lulu was flipping her shoes.

Nell stared at the Netherbeast. The cat blinked his yellow supernova eyes and lashed his tail at the commotion. How did he get into the car? She was *sure* he hadn't been here a second ago.

Lulu twisted around and glared at the black cat as the car veered wildly across its lane. "Where did you get—that thing looks like you found it in a dumpster!"

"I found him next to a dumpster," Nell said. "But I didn't bring him! He must have followed me. He likes blue raspberry slushies."

"I'm pulling over." They were just outside of downtown Cape Green, where the blocks of boutiques and restaurants began to turn into shabby office buildings, warehouses, and junkyards. Lulu slid her car into a gravel turnoff and switched off the engine. "Okay, no. It's gone. Put it out, now."

"I can't leave him *here!*" Nell said.

Lulu hopped out of the car and pulled open Nell's door. "I'm not having this conversation. The alley cat goes. You can be weird on your *own* time and in your *own* car."

"That's *just* like you," Nell said. *Weird.* That was the worst thing anybody could be, according to Lulu. Mom and Barb agreed with her. Nell felt her face getting hot. All the Tick People in Deer Valley were probably going to think she was super weird, too.

Lulu threw up her hands. "Look, I *need* this job. Cape Green is stuffed to the gills with high school students who've already landed all the summer jobs available. And you need to prove you're ready to be a Junior Volunteer. That means Aunt Jerry *has* to think we're responsible. And that doesn't include surprise feral cats!"

"He's not feral exactly," Nell said, but her shoulders slumped. Lulu was kind of right. ". . . Okay. But we have to bring him back to the mini-mart where he lives. He doesn't deserve to be abandoned in an overgrown warehouse parking lot."

"We're already late, thanks to you," Lulu barked, but she seemed a little less rabid. She slid back into the driver's seat. "Let that cat out here or you're not coming."

Nell crossed her arms. "Fine, I'm not coming. You can just stay in high school *forever*."

Lulu leaned back and put a hand to her forehead. She looked like Barb when she did that. Put-upon.

They sat in silence for a few moments.

"Mom and Barb will never let you have a cat," Lulu said.

Nell shrugged. "We'll be in Deer Valley all summer. I can find a home for him there."

Lulu snorted. "Yeah. Good luck. I'm sure people will be lining up to adopt that thing."

Nell didn't say anything. Lulu was kind of right, again. The Netherbeast thrust a scraggly back leg into the air and started cleaning his butt with a loud slurping sound.

Finally, Lulu looked back. "Ugh," she muttered, "it smells."

"He needs a bath," Nell said.

"He needs a fumigation," Lulu said.

Nell slowly closed the back door.

After a moment, Lulu rolled her eyes and started the car again, the Netherbeast still bathing himself in the backseat. "This is on you. This is *all* on you. Aunt Jerry's probably severely allergic to garbage cats and she'll be dead ten minutes after we arrive. And I'll laugh as I'm handing you over to the police."

"It's a deal," Nell said as Lulu swung back out onto the street, cranking the music.

Nell pointed at the Netherbeast and lowered her voice. "And here's *our* deal: you have to be a cat. I don't know what you really are, but as long as we're in Deer Valley, you're a cat. You understand? A cat. *All the time.* Aunt Jerry will flip her shoes if she finds out that you're a—a—not a cat. And I need her to not flip her shoes. I need her to tell Mom and Barb and Shana that I'm the most responsible person in Deer Valley and to *not flip her shoes.*"

The Netherbeast nodded emphatically. He bounced to his feet. Then he skittered up the back window of the car like a cockroach and launched, flattening himself into a hairy pancake that floated back down to the seat.

Nell glanced at the front seat. Lulu was bobbing her head to the song, not paying attention.

"Cat!" Nell hissed at the Netherbeast pancake. He blinked his flat yellow eyes at her.

Then he popped back into cat shape and jumped,

for the first time ever,

into a lap.

Nell scratched between his gross ears. "That's better. Nice kitty." She wrinkled her nose. "Wow, Lulu and I actually agree on something, though. You're filthy."

The Netherbeast growled.

Nell cracked a smile. Sure, the Netherbeast was stinky and menacing and, okay, not exactly a *cat,* but . . .

But Nell had a pet! At least for a few weeks. And maybe, just *maybe,* if she could become a responsible Junior Volunteer, she could convince her parents that she was ready for her own pet— and that the Netherbeast was pleasant and tidy enough to live with them. She had all summer to prepare.

As she scratched the fur between his ears, the Netherbeast began to purr.

"Good boy," Nell said.

The Netherbeast purred louder and louder, until he was so loud that Lulu had to turn up the music. He stretched his long legs out across Nell's lap and purred a big, rumbly *glorp!* of happiness.

Brownish-green sludge glooped out of the Netherbeast's ears and slopped all over Nell's pants and the back seat of Lulu's car.

CHAPTER FIVE

THE ALBATROSS

Rose Cottage Bed & Breakfast
PART OF THE COZY CORNERS SISTERHOOD OF INNS (LLC)

That was what the charming sign out front with the painted pink roses said. Below it was stapled a notice: CLOSED FOR RENOVATIONS

Nell and Lulu stood at the end of the driveway and stared. The house didn't look anything like the Rose Cottage Nell remembered from her last visit. Somehow, Aunt Jerry's cozy B&B had become a rotten-wood and ragged-curtain kind of creepy. It looked like a fancy dollhouse that had been left in the yard all winter. Dead, brown pine needles coated the lawn, the front steps were basically rubble, and the gutters were hanging off the roof.

Rose Cottage was definitely an albatross.

"Does this place look a little . . . abandoned?" Nell set her suitcase down on the gravel. The air vibrated with birdsong and—something else. Music? Sappy, awful music?

Lulu crossed her arms. "It looks like Edgar Allan Poe barfed up a house."

It was true. Old clapboards hung crookedly off one wall, and leaves had settled in clusters over the rotten roof like Band-Aids. Patches of dirty white paint still clung to the trim of the open bay windows on the first floor. The small porch sagged, cracked like the smile of a skull. In the front garden, a concrete goat statue winced like it was having intestinal problems.

What had happened to Aunt Jerry's B&B?

The Netherbeast jumped out of the backseat of Lulu's car. He squatted, took a dump on the lawn, looked up at Rose Cottage, and *hissed*.

Lulu frowned at the Netherbeast. "Ugh, I knew we should have ditched that thing."

"MrowwWWWWW!" wailed the Netherbeast, his eyes flashing.

Nell's stomach was doing somersaults. "He doesn't like the house, I guess." *It's giving me the creeps, too,* she thought.

"Is anybody home?" Lulu trotted up the front steps and through the door, leaving Nell standing in the driveway. Nell picked up her suitcase and started to follow, but she stopped when she heard shouting from around the side of the house.

"This is too much!" An angry voice floated over the wild hedge that lined a path made of wide stones. A startled chipmunk scurried from a dry window box. Someone responded, but the voice cut them off. "A *week?* Absolutely not! I will not spend one more *second* in this house!"

With a *swish,* a woman in a white collared shirt emerged from behind the hedge and stormed down the path toward the driveway. She yanked a name tag off and threw it into the front yard. The movement caught the Netherbeast's attention. He began stalking the name tag like a lion on the savanna, hindquarters quivering.

Right behind the angry woman, a short lady in an army-green jacket came clonking down the stone path. Her shoes were very shiny. "You're making a poor decision," the green-jacket woman said. She had a severe looking face, as though she'd chosen to grow deep lines around her mouth instead of ever smiling. "If you walk now, you'll be blacklisted from the Cozy Corners Sisterhood of Inns for good."

"I don't care, Ms. Tipton!" the angry woman said. "We were just fine doing things Jerry's way, and then everything went bananas! And you waltz in here with a million *rules*—how many folds in the bath towels, how often to shine a name tag, how many flowers per square foot may grow in the garden! I'm surprised I'm allowed to brush my teeth the way I want to! Not to mention—" The woman gestured vaguely. "—The fake bird noises and nauseating elevator music you're piping over that loudspeaker!"

"The Cozy Corners Sisterhood has standards that need to be enforced," the woman in the green jacket, Ms. Tipton, said. "I realize this is an adjustment from the *chaos* that has been running rampant here, but—"

The woman pointed at Ms. Tipton. "Chaos, schmaos! I'm not leaving because of rules. You can throw rules at this place all you like, but both you and I know there's something *wrong* here. There's something *wrong* with this house, and you're a dingbat if you keep ignoring it!"

The Netherbeast made a *ding!* noise. He sounded just like an elevator. Nell shot him a look. "Meow," he said, innocently.

The woman in the white shirt raised her voice even more. "You and Jerry can find someone else to put up with this place. I quit!" She flounced off, crunching down the driveway and turning left onto the road toward town.

Ms. Tipton watched with her hands on her hips. Finally, she noticed Nell, who was standing perfectly still. "And who are *you?*" Ms. Tipton asked, peering suspiciously. "Some *hooligan*, planning to steal the pipes? Is that what you're doing? Waiting for your chance to steal the *pipes?* That's just what we need, on top of everything else."

Nell opened her mouth, but words didn't come out.

The Netherbeast came rolling across the driveway and flopped at Ms. Tipton's feet. She gave him a dirty look and said, "Ugh! Shoo! Get out of here, fleabag!"

"*Hhh! Hhh! Hrrrk!*" The Netherbeast puked a wet hairball onto Ms. Tipton's shiny shoes, streaking them black and green.

She glared at Nell. "Is this your cat?"

"Uh . . ."

"It's not polite to barf on people's shoes," Ms. Tipton said.

It's not polite to call people hooligans, either, Nell thought, looking at the ground.

The Netherbeast ignored Ms. Tipton. He pounced on the discarded name tag again and swallowed it in one gulp.

Lulu came trotting down the steps. "Aunt Jerry's not inside," she said. "Maybe around back."

"I don't want to steal the pipes," Nell muttered.

Lulu crossed her arms. "Can you not be completely gonzo for five seconds?"

"And here's another one!" Ms. Tipton said snippily.

"Oh!" Lulu wheeled around. "I—sorry, who are you?"

"Who are *you?*" Ms. Tipton snipped.

"Darlings!" A sunny voice interrupted them as someone came twirling out from behind the hedge and down the stone path. It was Aunt Jerry. She wore a shiny name tag like the one the Netherbeast had just eaten, which read *Geraldine Moufflon, Manager.* "You're here!" she said. "I'm so glad! I forgot you were coming today!"

With a *hork!*, the Netherbeast vomited again. A melted hunk of plastic squished from his mouth and lay smoldering in the grass. Nell stepped in front of it so the others wouldn't see.

Aunt Jerry was tall, even taller than Nell, and wore red cat-eye glasses coated with glitter. She was wrapped in a loud, flower-print dress that

didn't quite reach the tops of her high, high heels. Her short purple hair stuck out from her head in spikes.

It was hard for Nell to believe she was related to Mom, who wouldn't have been caught dead with spike hair or glitter glasses. Sisters could sure be different from each other. Nell and Lulu were proof of that.

"Hi, Aunt Jerry," Lulu said. Nell honked.

Ms. Tipton crossed her arms and looked at Aunt Jerry. "Friends of yours?"

Adi Rule

"Oh!" Aunt Jerry gave a start, as though she hadn't realized Ms. Tipton were standing there. "Why, yes. These are my nieces, Tallulah and Eleanor."

"Pleased to meet you." Lulu stuck out her hand, but Ms. Tipton didn't shake it. "We're here to help out."

"I certainly hope so." Ms. Tipton glanced at her watch. "I have to go. I have a video call. I'll be making my report on rule compliance as well as the *state* of these repairs." She wrinkled her nose at Rose Cottage as though it were a gigantic pile of dog poop.

Aunt Jerry's face fell. "We just need more *time*. The staff has . . ." She shot Lulu and Nell a nervous look as though she didn't want to finish her sentence.

"Then I suggest you find some new staff," Ms. Tipton said flatly. "You have your work cut out for you, Ms. Moufflon. We will make our final decision at the end of the month. Until then, I'll be observing your progress *closely* and sending reports. Goodbye." She strode over to a car as shiny as her shoes and plonked into the driver's seat.

What on earth is going on? Nell thought. Had all the employees quit? It sure seemed like it. Who was Ms. Tipton, and what decision was she going to make at the end of the month?

Nell decided she didn't like Ms. Tipton. The Netherbeast apparently felt the same way, because he had slithered over to her car and was now aiming a single razor-sharp claw at its rear tire. Nell shot him a look. *"No slashing tires!"* she hissed, low so the others couldn't hear.

The Netherbeast hissed back. His claw quivered closer to the inflated rubber tire. A drop of sunlight glimmered off its sharp point. *Ping!*

Nell pointed sternly and shook her head. The Netherbeast narrowed his eyes in annoyance, but retracted his claw.

"Huggies!" Aunt Jerry scurried over to her nieces. She put her hands up and jiggled them. "I hope you're not too worn out, sweethearts. What a long ride from the coast! Go inside and have a pee, and then we'll enjoy a relaxing beverage in the screenhouse. It's just around back. Like a little greenhouse with screens instead of glass and chairs instead of plants.

Actually, I should put some plants in there. They would look nice."

"Nell brought a cat," Lulu said. Nell gulped, but she didn't know what to say. As usual.

"Oh!" Aunt Jerry looked down at the Netherbeast, who was back to glaring at the house. His eyes were black marbles and his grubby fur stood on end. He looked like he could give you six diseases just by being in the same room. "Well!" Aunt Jerry said. "Is he from your shelter? I'm sure he's . . . Well, all quaint B&Bs need a resident kitty, right? I'm sure he'll be . . . well!" And she fluttered away down the flagstone path that curved around to the back of the house.

Lulu snorted. "She's as bonkers as you."

Nell didn't answer. She couldn't help staring at Rose Cottage's vine-covered bricks, rusty porch rail, and dark doorway. The house stared back through its cracked windows. What was it the angry woman had said? *There's something wrong here.*

But Nell kept quiet and put on a blank face. The last thing she wanted to do was show that she was, well—

Afraid. Afraid of this staring, broken-down house. She couldn't let on. Because the only thing worse than living in this creepy house all summer would be living in this creepy house with an older sister who thought you were a scaredy-cat.

Suddenly, a wave of cold came over her, popping prickles up and down her arms. Nell couldn't be sure of what happened next, but it seemed like Rose Cottage trembled. No, not a tremble—more like a *fluff.* Like a chicken aggressively fluffing its feathers. The clapboards puffed and the roof rippled. A few shingles dislodged and slid over the edge, landing with soft thuds in the dead grass.

Nell looked wide-eyed at Lulu, but her sister was checking her phone. She hadn't noticed.

Something in this house is angry, Nell thought. *Something doesn't want us here.*

✦ ✦ ✦

CHAPTER SIX

A VOICE IN THE DARK

Nell and Lulu set their suitcases down on the moth-eaten carpet in the dim foyer of Rose Cottage. The Netherbeast sat in the doorway, so frizzed out it looked like all his hairs were trying to escape in different directions.

Just inside, there was a little front counter with a computer where guests would check in. Only there were no guests right now—*Closed for Renovations,* the notice out front said.

There was a fancy staircase that led to the upstairs rooms, with a wide bannister that might be good for sliding if anyone ever had fun here, which seemed doubtful. To the left was a parlor filled with old furniture, and to the right was the kitchen. Past the staircase, Nell could see two more doors with brass knobs.

Lulu twisted the first knob; it was the bathroom. She pushed the squeaky door open and flipped on the light. Nell tried to get a look inside. "Me first, scuzzbag," her sister said, smacking the door shut in Nell's face. After a moment, a water pipe squealed *Eeeeeeeee!* like someone screaming.

Nell leaned against the age-darkened wallpaper. Rose Cottage felt like it had been decaying for decades. But she knew that wasn't true. They had visited only a few years ago, and the B&B had been filled with happy tourists, a couple of pleasant employees, and Aunt Jerry—beaming, flitting, friendly. People played cards in the parlor and made themselves flavored coffee in the kitchen. It had been a place full of conversation and relaxation.

What happened? Nell wondered. *Is it that awful Ms. Tipton? Or is the house itself driving people away?*

Nell ran her fingers along the dusty wainscoting. The Netherbeast was nowhere in sight, and Nell didn't blame him. Rose Cottage was dismal and airless and everything creaked. Who would want to stay here?

A glint caught Nell's eye. Across the hall hung a painting with a fancy wooden frame. The frame was pretty. The painting was not.

Nell hadn't noticed this picture before. Of course, there had been a lot more going on the last time she was here. She hadn't exactly spent her time mooning around in the hallway staring at the walls.

It was a portrait of an old man in a suit. His wispy white hair puffed out from his balding head and his bright eyes seemed to be looking everywhere and nowhere at once. His lined mouth was set in the deepest scowl Nell had ever seen. On the bottom of the frame was a little round plaque with the name *Eslick*.

If looks could kill, Nell thought.

Suddenly, a chill prickled her skin again, as though an icy gust had swept the hall. She whipped her head around. The front door was closed, dust motes swirling in the sunlight through its stained glass. Where was the breeze coming from? Was there a window open or something?

Nell crept farther down the hallway. Behind the front stairs, she found another door. Maybe a closet? She wiggled her toes in her sneakers. There was definitely a draft creeping out from underneath.

She reached for the black iron latch, the kind you grasp by the handle and press on the top with your thumb. The metal was electric cold. With a deep breath, she pressed the thumb-lever and pulled the door open.

For a second, Nell's breath froze in her lungs. There was no closet behind the door, but narrow, wooden stairs leading down into darkness. Nell reached in. She felt along the wall for a light switch. Nothing but cobwebs.

Cautiously, she took one step down, keeping her left fingers touching the door, running her right hand along the crumbling plaster wall in search of a switch. The darkness pooled around her ankles like frigid water.

Then she got that strange feeling again, as though there was something *angry* in the darkness below—invisible, but so close, she could practically feel it breathing.

"Exploring the basement?"

Lulu's voice made Nell jump. Then *slam!* The door banged shut behind her. Everything went black.

"Hey!" Nell pressed her shoulder into the door. She pounded on the wood. "Let me out!" She could hear her sister laughing as she struggled to keep the door closed from the other side.

Nell scratched and pushed. She tried not to think about the big, black space below her. She *definitely* tried not to think about what might be hiding there. Her heart thumped in her ears.

Then, another sound crawled into her ears: a voice she had never heard before. A whisper, feathery and copper and cold and plain as day.

"Byron . . ."

Nell shrieked. "Lulu!" She pummeled the door with her fists. *"Lulu!"*

The door gave. Lulu had stepped out of the way, and Nell went tumbling back into the hallway, landing flat on her face on the musty carpet.

Lulu was cackling like a goose.

CHAPTER SEVEN

IT'S A DUMP

Nell could have shoved her awful, squawking sister right over backward, but she was too shaken up by the whispery voice in the dark.

"Whoa there, tiger!" Lulu lazily dodged Nell's flailing arms. "So afraid of the scary basement! Wooooo!" She laughed and started back down the hallway to the front door.

Nell followed. Her fists were still balled but she glued them to her sides. She couldn't *admit* she'd been scared of the basement—not unless she wanted her jerk of a sister to trap her down there again. But she couldn't shake the sound. *Byron . . .*

What did it mean?

They found the screenhouse out back in the middle of a brambly, overgrown garden. Inside, Aunt Jerry was reclining on a cushioned bench, sipping lemonade. "Sit down, sit down, lovies!"

She gestured to a silver tray set with a pitcher and two glasses. "Have a bev! Sippy sip!" Her voice wobbled.

Lulu stepped in front of Nell, helping herself. "Thank you, Aunt Jerry," she said sweetly.

"I'm so glad you girls are here to help out," Aunt Jerry said as Lulu hogged the comfiest looking chair. "I need all the help I can get right now, I'm afraid."

"Is it something to do with Ms. Tipton?" Lulu asked.

"It—yes," Aunt Jerry said. She put her lemonade on the floor and sat up. "We simply *must*

Adi Rule

impress Ms. Tipton, my girls. We must all be on
our best behavior. You see, Ms. Tipton is from the
Cozy Corners Sisterhood of Inns, LLC. They own
Rose Cottage. And a lot of other places."

"I thought you owned Rose Cottage?" Nell
asked, balancing on a rickety stool. Her lemonade
sploshed onto her pants.

"Aunt Jerry only *manages* Rose Cottage,"
Lulu said. "That means she's in charge of it."

"I know what 'manages' means," Nell
muttered.

"Yes, well, I might not be in charge for much
longer." Aunt Jerry shook her fingers nervously,
like she was playing an invisible harp. "It's all
because of the Flying Florentines. Oh, I wish
they'd never made a reservation!"

Lulu gasped. "The Flying Florentines are
coming *here?*"

Aunt Jerry raised her purple eyebrows. "In
three weeks," she whispered.

Nell frowned. "Who are the Flying
Florentines?"

Lulu rolled her eyes. "Seriously? *Seriously,*
Nell?"

"They're travel influencers," Aunt Jerry said. She looked horrified.

"They're *the* travel influencers," Lulu said. "They have over three million followers."

"Oh!" Aunt Jerry cried, clutching her collar. Nell blinked. "That sounds like a lot of followers." Lulu rolled her eyes again. Nell hoped they'd get stuck like that.

"Not to mention Barb is *obsessed* with them," Lulu said. "Remember when she put those glass vases full of rocks all over the house and everybody kept tripping over them?"

"Yeah," Nell said with a shudder, remembering the Summer of Stubbed Toes.

"It's because the Florentines posted all these pictures of vases of rocks at this hotel they were gushing about," Lulu said. "Then all their followers filled their houses up with the things."

Aunt Jerry looked through the screened windows at the wild garden and gulped. "When they booked a room—it was unbelievable! The Flying Florentines, in my bed and breakfast!" Her voice was high and trembly. "They're so important, Ms. Tipton personally came all the way out here to make sure Rose Cottage was in tip-top shape for their arrival. And then . . . everything went wrong."

"Why?" asked Nell.

"I have no idea!" Aunt Jerry's knees trembled under her flower-print dress. "It was fine at first. Mostly fine. The Sisterhood has a lot of rules that, uh, we weren't always following."

"Like how to fold the towels," Nell said.

"Right," Aunt Jerry said anxiously. "Left roll, right roll, backward in half, double forward . . . or was it *right* roll, then backward . . . oh, *dear*, I think it might *start* with the double forward . . ."

Nell cleared her throat.

"Yes, well, anyway." Aunt Jerry snapped out of her towel nightmare. "Ms. Tipton also insisted on all the curtains being washed, the wallpaper scrubbed, cleaning out old junk, replacing the outlet covers. The staff and I worked all day long, besides taking care of the guests. But suddenly, last week—it's like the house just self-destructed!" Her voice became small. "We had to close down to try to get everything fixed in time for the Florentines. We should be so much further along by now with the repairs. It's just—so many things keep going wrong."

"It's an old house," Lulu said. "Old houses have issues."

But Nell thought about the falling shingles, the screaming water pipes—and the voice in the basement. Rose Cottage wasn't just an old house. It was a house with an attitude.

Aunt Jerry's gaze was far away. "Cracks in the walls, those are normal. A bit of rot." She gulped. "The—the piano exploding . . . that was a little unexpected . . ." She leaned forward, her voice urgent. "If the Florentines don't have a good time at Rose Cottage . . . if they think it's a dump, I'm afraid the Cozy Corners Sisterhood of Inns will close us for good."

"Don't worry," Lulu said. "We'll get it all fixed up. Rose Cottage will charm the pants off the Flying Florentines! Right, Nell?"

Nell nodded. But she understood why Aunt Jerry was terrified that the Florentines would think Rose Cottage was a dump.

Because it was.

CHAPTER EIGHT
CATS DON'T MELT

Nell, Lulu, and Aunt Jerry spent the afternoon planting what felt like eight thousand purple zinnias in the front beds of Rose Cottage. All the flowers Aunt Jerry had planted earlier in the spring had shriveled and died. Planting the new flowers was tedious work because they had to stick to the Sisterhood rules, which required perfectly straight rows and exactly six-inch spacing between plants.

When they were done, Lulu ordered a pizza and the three of them sat on the front porch to wait for the delivery. Nell and Aunt Jerry shared the porch swing and Lulu perched dreamily on top of the wide wooden railing. The warm breeze tickled their tired arms and the sunlight made patterns on the lawn. It was a nice evening.

Well, it was nice until the Netherbeast rolled in, covered in muck and smelling like death. He oozed onto the swing and plopped down with a *spluck* between Nell and Aunt Jerry.

"Oh!" Aunt Jerry said. "Nelly's kitty! Were you exploring? Aren't you handsome!" She reached out and started to scratch between the cat's ears.

The Netherbeast's eyes rolled upwards, as though he could see the fingers scratching the top of his own head. His black pupils expanded. *Delicious fingers.* As Nell watched, his long fangs started to grow and glisten . . .

No! Nell panicked. She cleared her throat to get the Netherbeast's attention. Then she muttered sharply, "Be a cat!"

"What?" Aunt Jerry asked, startled.

Nell blinked. "Uh. I said, 'He's a cat!'"

"Oh," Aunt Jerry looked confused. "Yes."

Lulu gave Nell a look. Neither she nor Aunt Jerry noticed the Netherbeast's fangs growing longer and longer . . .

"Yes." Nell shot a penetrating stare at the Netherbeast. "He's a *cat*."

The Netherbeast glared at her.

Nell glared back.

Then, with a snort, the glistening fangs went back to normal. The Netherbeast closed his eyes. After a moment, he began to purr, as though he were just some regular kitty getting his head scratched instead of a finger-hungry monstrosity.

"I don't remember you having a kitty last time I visited," Aunt Jerry said, picking something gross out of her nail that she'd scraped off the Netherbeast's head. "Where did you get him?"

Lulu snorted. Nell ignored her. "Uh—he was a stray," she said.

"It probably has garbage rabies," Lulu said. "As soon as we're home in Cape Green, it's going back to its dumpster."

The Netherbeast purred extra loudly and flipped onto his back.

"Ohhh!" Aunt Jerry squeaked, tickling his tum. "Well, I don't mind kitties. If they're well behaved, that is." She gave a nervous laugh. "Some cats are *strange,* don't you think? My neighbor Mr. Denver had an old cat who liked to lick plastic bags. It would pull them out of the drawers in the kitchen and lick them all day long, *slrrrip, slrrrip, slrrrip!*" She shivered. "It gave me the creeps! I couldn't set *foot* in that house, not with that weird, bag-licking cat. I would have just fainted into a heap."

Nell started to sweat. *Fragile.* That was how Barb described Aunt Jerry. The sort of person you spoke to with a smile and a soft voice. Definitely not the sort of person you introduced to a Netherbeast.

"The front yard looks a lot better with the flowers," Nell said, trying to distract from the weird cat. The Netherbeast purred and fluffed.

"It's a travesty. The hedges are completely overgrown." Aunt Jerry sighed. "But a snip here, a snip there . . ." She looked up hopefully. "Do you think?"

"Oh—yeah," Nell said. Aunt Jerry didn't notice Lulu's skeptical expression. Nell agreed with her sister. It was going to take a lot more than a few snips to get Rose Cottage back to the way it was—and Aunt Jerry, too.

"Nell said she wants to personally dig up all the poison ivy," Lulu said, leaning back against a porch post. Nell made a face at her.

"Good. Yes." Aunt Jerry smiled weakly. "The Cozy Corners Sisterhood of Inns, LLC, has a strict rule against all poison ivy. There *is* a lot of it, isn't there? And it's never grown here before . . . especially not in the bathtubs . . ."

Nell rubbed the Netherbeast's tummy. His furry body flattened over the swing's slats.

"Ms. Moufflon?" a voice called. "Hello?" A boy came trotting up the driveway carrying a gallon of paint. He was wearing faded overalls and looked about Nell's age.

"Bucky, how nice," Aunt Jerry said. "Come meet the family."

The boy's eyes widened. He clearly hadn't been expecting to meet the family. "I, uh, I'm just dropping this off on my way home. So we can paint the door tomorrow."

"Girls, this is my neighbor, Bucky Denver." Aunt Jerry beckoned until Bucky awkwardly approached the porch. "His dad's company is taking care of the big repairs on Rose Cottage. And Bucky's helping me out with some odd jobs!"

There was an uncomfortable silence while everyone waited for Bucky to say something. But all he did was stare at the ground. Nell understood how he felt.

"These are my nieces, Tallulah and Eleanor," Aunt Jerry said.

Lulu smiled. "Hey, there!" She was trying to be nice, which was annoying, since she never tried to be nice to Nell.

"Nice to meet you," Nell muttered.

Bucky mumbled about paint. There was something mooselike about him, Nell thought.

A car rumbled up the driveway and slid to a stop. Ms. Tipton had returned from her video call. Nell noticed Aunt Jerry stiffen, and remembered her aunt's words: *We must all be on our best behavior.* Now, Nell understood. Ms. Tipton was a *spy,* looking for any reason at all to close Aunt Jerry's beloved Rose Cottage for good. But why? Shouldn't Ms. Tipton *want* the Famous Whoevers to have a good time here?

The spy slid out of her car, brushing dust off her pants. "Must be nice to have time to laze around on the porch."

"Don't the flowers look pretty?" Lulu asked.

Ms. Tipton gave the zinnias a critical eye. "Let's hope they last this time." She crossed her arms. "That front door is an embarrassment."

Aunt Jerry gave a nervous laugh. "Yes. All the paint just sort of . . . fell off it. Last week." She made an explosion gesture. "Foomp!"

"*Fell off* it?" Ms. Tipton shook her head. "It's a shame the Cozy Corners Sisterhood of Inns, LLC, hasn't been keeping a better eye on this place. It's clear that Rose Cottage has been terribly neglected for quite some time." She clicked her tongue. "Frankly, I think this is all due to gross mismanagement."

"I assure you," said Aunt Jerry, the blood draining from her face, "Rose Cottage was perfectly fine until last week! Until just after you arrived!"

Ms. Tipton made an angry squeak. "Are you *accusing* me of something?"

"No!" Aunt Jerry held up her hands. "It's just that this—all *this*—has never happened before! I don't know what to make of it. It's positively supernatural!"

"I'll stop you right there." Ms. Tipton barked, pointing. The tip of her finger was half an inch from Aunt Jerry's nose. "I do not want to hear the word *supernatural* again. Rose Cottage has not been well taken care of, and that's that. If I find *any* funny business—" Here she glared at each person one by one, including Bucky, who seemed as though he might faint. "—If *any of you* are up to any *funny business*, I'll have the Sisterhood CEO on the phone faster than you can say 'out of business.' We do not put up with any shenanigans in this outfit. And we definitely do not employ weirdos!"

Weirdos. There was that word again. Nell swallowed. Even though Ms. Tipton's gaze hadn't lingered on her any longer than anybody else, she felt put on the spot. Not only was she too weird for the Cape Green Companion Animal Shelter, now her weirdness might put Aunt Jerry's whole livelihood in jeopardy. *I will not be weird,* she told herself. *I will be mature. I will be on my best behavior. I will show Shana and Ms. Tipton and everybody else that I am a regular kid who is capable of helping out at a regular bed and breakfast and being a regular Junior Volunteer.*

Then, suddenly, Nell's fingers felt . . . strange. Just a moment ago, she'd been absentmindedly scratching the Netherbeast's tummy. Now, she looked down to where the cat was relaxing on the swing between her and Aunt Jerry. And almost screamed.

In his ecstasy, the Netherbeast had melted.

That wasn't a figure of speech—the black cat was *liquid*, a gross, furry puddle that spread over the seat and dripped between the wooden slats onto the porch floor.

Nell jerked her hand away. "Eew!" Thinking fast, she slid the throw blanket from the back of the swing over the Netherpuddle, hiding it from view.

"Oh!" Aunt Jerry said, whipping her head around.

Lulu scowled. "What's the matter with you?"

Nell laughed nervously. "Nothing. Bug."

Ms. Tipton squinted, looking around. "I thought you just cleaned up this porch."

"Don't worry," Lulu said. "Nell probably brought bugs in on her. They live in her ears." She clapped her hands. "Anyway, Ms. Tipton, I was thinking about some stone cherubs . . ." And she was chattering at Ms. Tipton as though they were old pals.

Nell was grudgingly grateful to her sister for the distraction. She knew Lulu was just drawing Ms. Tipton's attention away because Nell was too strange, but it was a relief anyway. Nell lifted the corner of the blanket and gave the Netherbeast a harsh look. "No!" she whispered.

Two yellow eyeballs floating in fur soup opened inquisitively.

Nell glanced at Aunt Jerry, but her head was turned away. She was engrossed in the conversation. Nell leaned down and kept her whisper as quiet as possible. "Pull yourself together!" She pointed at the Netherpuddle. "*Cats don't melt.*"

The yellow eyes blinked, skeptical. Globs of black hair dribbled onto the floor. Nell covered the goo back up with the blanket.

". . . forsythia. Do you think so, Nelly?" Aunt Jerry reached across the bench and gave Nell's hair a scruff.

"Nothing!" Nell said. "I mean!" She put a firm hand on the throw blanket. "I mean, yeah. Forsythia. Definitely." Nell had no idea what forsythia was.

All of a sudden, Ms. Tipton sniffed. She squinted. "What's that smell?"

Nell gagged. Nothing like the scent of liquid Netherbeast in your nostrils. "No idea," she croaked.

Now everybody was sniffing. "There is *something,* isn't there?" Aunt Jerry said.

"Like a swamp," Bucky murmured.

"Or like something died under the floorboards," Ms. Tipton said.

Lulu held her nose. "Ugh! It's probably Nell's gross cat."

Aunt Jerry's eyebrows jumped up. "Oh, is the kitty okay?" She reached for the throw blanket covering the hairy puddle that used to be the Netherbeast.

Nell's heart almost stopped. "No!" she screamed, grabbing the blanket. "Don't touch that!"

Aunt Jerry was so startled by the outburst, she screamed, too. Lulu swore and almost fell off the railing. Bucky jumped six inches into the air. Ms. Tipton's eyes flashed like daggers.

Everyone was looking at Nell.

"Uh," she began. "I mean—don't touch the blanket because the cat's sleeping under there."

"After you shrieked in its ears?" Lulu said.

"I like cats," Bucky said in a frail voice.

"There is something very *weird* going on here," Ms. Tipton said. She elbowed her way around Nell's body and grasped the throw blanket. "What are you hiding?"

And she yanked the blanket away. Nell gasped.

Underneath, a perfectly average cat was curled up on the bench, fast asleep.

CHAPTER NINE

THE FIRST NIGHT

Nell dragged her suitcase up the back stairs from the kitchen. It bumped against dry wood treads, worn to curves by years of use. The Netherbeast rode on her shoulders, draping himself like a shawl.

"Oof." Nell yanked the suitcase around a narrow corner and almost fell over. The Netherbeast obnoxiously wrapped his long tail around her eyes.

Nell swatted the tail away. "I can't see. Cut it out." The Netherbeast hissed. He moved his tail out of Nell's eyes, but gained ten pounds, just to be cranky.

Lulu was already in their new room. Her stuff was spread out all over one of the beds, on the side with more outlets *and* the window.

"You can't use my outlets," Lulu said.

Nell put her hands on her hips. "Well, *you* can't use *my*—" She looked around her side of the room. "—baseboard heater."

"You can smooch your baseboard heater in the moonlight and call it a love story," Lulu said, flapping the mustiness out of her bedsheets.

The Netherbeast dropped onto Nell's bedside table with a *THUMP.* A white ceramic lamp wobbled.

"Can you keep that thing under control?" Lulu asked.

The Netherbeast ballooned up until he was practically a beach ball. Nell stuck out her tongue and made a fart noise. Lulu pretended not to notice. They all went to bed without saying goodnight.

But Nell couldn't sleep. She kept thinking about the voice in the cellar. *That* was the key to why the house suddenly started falling apart, she was sure—and the key to fixing it. There was something angry down there in the basement.

But what could she do about it? Nell couldn't imagine Aunt Jerry being any help. She'd probably just say, "Oh!" and clutch her collar. And they couldn't ask Ms. Tipton to investigate. She'd hit the roof if anybody said the word *supernatural* again.

Maybe Nell had to figure this out on her own. She was good at solving mysteries, after all. Okay, she usually tackled lost pet mysteries, not haunted house mysteries, but what was the difference? Observe, learn, connect the dots.

Byron, the voice had whispered. What did it mean? And *who had said it?*

The light and dark shapes on the wallpaper looked like floating faces in the gloom. Nell's foot was sticking out from under the blanket, hovering over the floor. She pulled it in. Nell had never been afraid of the dark, but frankly, Rose Cottage was creeping her out.

What if she and Lulu and Aunt Jerry were in danger?

The air felt fuzzy, like an all-over vibration in the background of Nell's mind. Like a coating of wax on her skin as thin as a bee's whisper.

She lay in bed, listening. Her ears strained over the sound of Lulu's white noise machine. Suddenly, a strange, wobbly sound, low and shuddering, started very close by.

Nell sat up, her heart thumping. Where was it coming from? Then she realized: the white ceramic lamp on her bedside table was trembling—all by itself.

The light from electronic things charging cast a dull murkiness over the room. Nell stared at the lamp. And as she watched, the tremors grew bigger and wider. Now the lamp was wobbling so much she was afraid it would topple over. Holding her breath, Nell reached out a hand—

"Stupid cat!" Lulu's voice cut through the racket. The rattling stopped.

Nell pulled her hand back and looked down. There was the Netherbeast on the rug next to her bed. His leg was raised and frozen mid-scratch, pressed up against the base of her bedside table. After a second, he started scratching again—*fwit-fwit-fwit-fwit-fwit*. The table juddered. The lamp wobbled.

"Go be itchy somewhere else!" Lulu snapped, tossing a dirty sock onto the Netherbeast's head. Offended, the cat sauntered over to an armchair and began clawing at the upholstery.

Lulu pulled her comforter over her head. "Sheesh, I thought we were having an earthquake."

"Yeah," Nell said, her heart rate returning to normal. "Uh, me, too."

CHAPTER TEN

AN AWKWARD BREAKFAST

Nell *had* to say something about the voice in the basement.

Didn't she?

She peered at Lulu over a box of Corn Bran. The kitchen was awash in morning sunlight. It reminded Nell of a playhouse, with its frilly curtains and matching decorative pots hung above the island. There was a twisty mini-chandelier over the sink that looked like birds. It was plain to see that this kitchen had once been a homey place for weary travelers—until Rose Cottage got haunted, or cursed, or both.

Lulu chewed a waffle while she played *Dragon Lords* on her phone. The game *beeped* and *whooshed* as she swiped and tapped the screen.

The Netherbeast was trying to sleep on Nell's feet. When one of Lulu's electronic dragons roared, the grouchy cat would screech like a chickadee sticking its beak into Nell's ear. *Roar! SKREEK! Roar! SKREEK!*

But Nell wasn't thinking about the noise. Instead, she closed her eyes tight. *What do you want, house?* she thought. She might even have said it out loud, just a little bit. *Who is Byron?*

All of a sudden, one of the light bulbs in the bird chandelier exploded, showering glass into the sink.

Nell jumped. The Netherbeast was so startled that he exploded, too, but just for a second.

Lulu barely looked up. "Great," she muttered, like hostile light fixtures were uncool.

"This sure is a strange house, huh?" Nell asked. She didn't want to be the first person to say *haunted.*

"You fit right in," Lulu said. *Roar!* went her phone. From the floor, the Netherbeast chirped, *SKREEK!* against Nell's eardrums.

Fine, Nell thought. If Lulu was going to be monosyllabic this morning (surprise), Nell would have to poke harder. "With everything Aunt Jerry said about all the stuff that's been happening . . .

Do you get the feeling that, you know, we're not . . . alone?"

The last shard of light bulb fell into the sink with sharp *crack*. A blue snap of electricity arced from the chandelier. For a split second, it looked like a scowling face hung in the air. Then it was gone.

Nell gasped. "Lulu?"

Her sister didn't answer; she was staring at her phone: *swipe, swipe, whoosh! Tap-tap-tap-tap—ROAR!* "Ha!" Lulu grunted. "Not alone? What do you mean?"

Nell wasn't sure what to say. It was apparently too much to hope Lulu had noticed any creepy voices or exploding light bulbs or, you know, an angry electric ghost face appearing over the breakfast table.

Lulu looked up at Nell, whose eyes were still wide with shock. "No, no, no," she said, leaning forward. "You are *not* starting some oddball . . . *thing* here in Deer Valley. Ms. Tipton will flip her shoes. And Aunt Jerry is far too fragile."

"But this house!" Nell said. "The light bulb just now! Can't you feel—"

"What we do *not*—" Lulu clattered her phone onto the table and pointed. "Okay, okay, listen, what we do *not need* right now is you getting *weird*."

"I'm not weird," Nell grumbled.

"You need to keep it together," Lulu snapped. She lowered her voice, looking nervously around as though poor Aunt Jerry might come tottering in at any moment and immediately collapse from all of Nell's weirdness. "Look, I try my best with you, Nell. When you don't get invited to stuff, or spend days at a time at the animal shelter, or *bark* at *strangers,* I try to defuse the situation. You know that. But Aunt Jerry is not like the kids at school, or the people in Cape Green. She's *fragile*."

Nell felt her teeth grinding. "Well, then, she's definitely not going to like the fact that this house is haunted!"

Lulu squeezed her eyes closed and *sighed*.

"I know what I heard," Nell said. She tried to be confident. Her voice came out like the bleat of a lost moose.

Lulu kept her eyes closed tight, as though if she wished hard enough, her little sister would disappear.

So that's what Nell did. She pushed her chair back, dropped her dish into the sink, and stomped out. The Netherbeast followed, stomping in her footsteps. His cement-heavy paws rattled Rose Cottage from its creepy attic all the way to its creepy basement.

CHAPTER ELEVEN

A FIVE-STAR REVIEW

Nell heard the *tap-tap-tap* **of a laptop from the** dining room down the hall. With a sickening flop of her stomach, Nell realized: fragile or not, Aunt Jerry might be the only person who would listen.

Should she tell her aunt about the ghost voice in the basement?

No.

Definitely not.

But what if Aunt Jerry knew who Byron was? What if she could help? Wouldn't Aunt Jerry want to know what was wrong with Rose Cottage, so they might have a chance of fixing it before the Cozy Sisterhood shut them down?

Nell headed for the dining room. The Netherbeast jumped onto her shoulders. It was like getting hit with a sack of warm, wet cement.

"Oof!" she grunted. "You're going to break my back, you tub."

The wet cement oozed up her neck and came to rest lightly on the top of her head, weighing no more than a piece of paper. Nell caught sight of herself in the hall mirror. The black cat was curled up like a coonskin cap, his long tail flowing behind her.

"That's better," she said, squinting. "I guess." Most people didn't wear their cats on their heads, but she had bigger things to worry about than most people's fashion choices.

Aunt Jerry was at the dining room table typing something. She didn't look up as Nell came in.

Nell grabbed a banana out of the fruit bowl and sat down. "Hey, Aunt Jerry."

"Oh!" Aunt Jerry noticed Nell with a start. "Nelly, I'm just . . . well, I'm just researching."

Nell scooted her chair over and took a look at the laptop screen. It was a slick page, full of colorful pictures and eye-catching posts. *The Flying Florentines.* They sounded like trapeze artists, not travel influencers.

Scanning the pictures, Nell didn't feel particularly influenced. Everything was too *perfect.* Perfect grass and trees. Perfect beaches. Tiny perfect baked goods, perfectly baked. So these were the famous Flying Florentines. Nell didn't know what to say. It seemed impossible that Rose Cottage or anyone in it could ever be perfect enough for them, ghost or no ghost.

"The back porch fell off last night," Aunt Jerry murmured. "Just . . . fell off. It made this *thppbt* sound. I mean, we don't really need a back porch, but—it seemed okay yesterday, you know?" She sighed. "And they're coming." It was like she was talking about an unstoppable horde of giant fire ants instead of a smiling couple wearing kooky sunglasses on a mountain summit. "Lulu is the new Assistant Manager, of course, but we need a housekeeper, a front desk person . . ."

"I can help out," Nell said. "Don't worry!"

"I wish they had never called," Aunt Jerry said forlornly. "Everything was fine before the Florentines made that reservation. Then the Cozy Corners Sisterhood of Inns, LLC, had to go and panic about *improvements.* The sisterhood hadn't shown up here in *years!*"

"The Florentines will love it," Nell said, hoping that wasn't a lie. "If we can just . . ."

Aunt Jerry's sparkly red glasses wobbled. "If we can just what?" She sounded terrified.

Nell gulped. "If we can just, you know, get the repairs done. I'm sure Mr. Denver will get everything back on track."

Aunt Jerry relaxed a little. "Yes." She pushed her glasses back up onto her nose. "He's doing a fine job. We still have time." She smiled.

Nell tried to smile back. "Yep." She took a deep breath. Her next words came shooting out all in a row. "Also-I-think-there's-a-ghost-in-the-basement."

Aunt Jerry's mouth fell open. Her eyes grew as round and white as pool balls with dots drawn in the middle. ". . . What?" she whispered.

Nell panicked. "What?" she said back.

"Did—did you say—" Aunt Jerry started, her words bobbling.

"I, um, I said that—"

"*GHOST?*" Aunt Jerry screeched, making the Netherbeast jump four feet into the air and land on his back in the middle of the table. "Here?" She clutched the collar of her flowered blouse. Her teeth started chattering. "The HR representative *promised!* I said I wouldn't *set foot* in a house with ghosts!" She fell back against her chair, breathing heavily. "Oh, oh, Nelly! Did you really . . . in the basement? Oh, goodness, we'll have to close forever! I'll have to move to Norway! Oh, what will we do?"

Nell felt as frozen as the Netherbeast, who was staring at Aunt Jerry with huge black eyes. Aunt Jerry hyperventilated and moaned and squeezed her collar. The Netherbeast backed away from the distressed, purple-haired woman. He crept behind Nell's uneaten banana,

   inch by inch,

     curling up,

       then slowly, *slowly,*

        shrinking

         and turning yellow,

until there was one more banana sitting quietly in the fruit bowl.

Aunt Jerry didn't even notice. In fact, she was squinting critically at Nell. "Is it . . ." she whispered. "Is it because of *you?*"

Nell blinked. "Me? What?"

Aunt Jerry pointed a shaking finger. "It's *you!* You brought ghosts with you!"

"*What?*" Nell's jaw dropped. "Aunt Jerry, Lulu and I just got here! The problems with Rose Cottage started last week; you said so yourself. We just came for Lulu's summer job!"

But Aunt Jerry widened her eyes and frowned even more deeply.

A slithery voice startled them. "Summer job? Ah, yes. Your sister." Ms. Tipton stood in the doorway. "But you need something, too, don't you, Eleanor?"

Nell gulped. Then she honked.

Ms. Tipton was looking down at a manila folder in her hands. "I have a form here from someone named Shana Jackson at the Cape Green Companion Animal Shelter." She held up some papers and peered at them. "Apparently, she requires a reference from Rose Cottage for *you,* Nell, before she allows you to become something called a 'Junior Volunteer.'" Ms. Tipton pointed and smiled. She had a lot of white teeth. "And here's where the signature goes. *My* signature."

"What?" Nell looked from Ms. Tipton to her aunt. "Aunt Jerry's supposed to do that."

Ms. Tipton shoved the papers back into the folder. "I don't think so," she said. "As Geraldine's superior, you are all working for *me*. So I get to decide if you are responsible enough to earn a reference or not."

All Nell could manage was shocked silence. One of the bananas in the fruit bowl gave Ms. Tipton a dirty look.

"But," Ms. Tipton said, "I will happily sign this form for you, Eleanor."

Nell was suspicious. "Really?"

"Of course," Ms. Tipton said. "Once the Florentines have enjoyed their stay here—and once they post a five-star review for Rose Cottage. That will make the Cozy Corners Sisterhood of Inns, LLC, very happy."

"Five stars?" Nell spluttered. "That's the most stars you can have!"

Ms. Tipton snapped the folder closed. "It is a tall order, isn't it? But the Sisterhood is very concerned about this place. *Very* concerned. So I'll tell you now—a five-star review is the only thing that's going to get you your reference, save your sister's job, and stop Rose Cottage from being shut down for good."

"Ms. Tipton!" Aunt Jerry squeaked.

Ms. Tipton smiled. "I guess we'd better get to work!" And she breezed out of the room.

Nell gaped at Aunt Jerry. "Are you going to let her do that?" she asked, exasperated. "I need that reference form signed!"

"Oh," Aunt Jerry squinted into her memory. "Oh, yes, the paperwork. Your parents did send that along, didn't they? I don't know how Ms. Tipton got ahold of it." She crossed her arms. "Well, the Florentines simply *must* have a good time, then. They must! For you girls!"

"Uh . . . what do you mean?" Nell asked. "I mean, we'll do everything we can to make sure the Florentines enjoy Rose Cottage, but obviously we can't *guarantee*—"

Aunt Jerry sat up very straight. "Guarantee? We *must* guarantee. Ms. Tipton said so."

"But . . . but that's bananas!" Nell stammered. One of the bananas nodded in agreement. "You're the real boss, Aunt Jerry. If I work hard, if I'm responsible, couldn't you vouch for me?"

"Oh, no!" Aunt Jerry said, horrified. "No, no, no. Ms. Tipton is in charge. I'm afraid I couldn't possibly sign your papers." She gripped the edge of the table so tightly her fingernails turned white. "That would be *fraud!*"

Nell's jaw dropped. Junior Volunteers would go out the window if the Flying Florentines didn't leave Rose Cottage a *five-star review?* Even without the haunted basement, Rose Cottage was hardly a luxury resort. How could they possibly do this? How could Aunt Jerry do this to them?

Nell looked at her aunt's lined face and wild eyes. And she realized that Aunt Jerry's dreams were riding on the Florentines, too. For the first time, Nell understood the word "fragile." There was something precarious and delicate inside Aunt Jerry, like a sliver of white porcelain running the length of her spine. Nell knew that if the review were a flop, if Rose Cottage had to close, that delicate thing inside Aunt Jerry would shatter along with everything else.

Too bad there was an angry voice in the basement and a Netherbeast in the fruit bowl.

Aunt Jerry crossed her arms. "I'll tell you one thing, Eleanor: I will *not* vouch for anyone who has brought *ghosts* and *weirdness* into this house!"

Nell swallowed. *If Aunt Jerry only knew how much weirdness I've brought with me. And right now it's disguised as a banana.* She panicked. She had to fix this. "Coats!" she blurted.

Aunt Jerry swiveled her pool ball eyes. "What?"

"Before, when I was talking about the basement—"

"You said *ghost!*"

"Oh, no," Nell said. "You thought I said 'ghost'?" Nell tried to laugh. It sounded like a moose drowning. "No, I said, 'coats.' I saw, like, a ton of gross old coats down there. We've got to get rid of them."

Aunt Jerry blinked. ". . . Coats? There aren't any coats in the basement." She frowned. "Or *are* there?" She looked at the ceiling, searching her mind. "Are there coats in the basement?"

"I mean, I *thought* there were," Nell said. "Maybe I'm thinking of something else."

Aunt Jerry's breathing was returning to normal. She reached out and patted Nell's hand. "Thank you for bringing it up. Of course we can't leave any old coats lying around. The Florentines absolutely detest extraneous soft goods in their environment. We'll be sure to tidy up. I started to fix it up down there when Ms. Tipton first got here, but I got sidetracked by everything else."

"Great!" Nell said. *Great,* she thought. *Aunt Jerry is more frightened of ghosts than any other human being on the entire planet and I just convinced her to go rummaging around in the haunted basement. What will she think about that?*

What will the Flying Florentines think about it?

And that was the moment Nell realized: If Aunt Jerry was too terrified even to give Nell a reference, how on earth would she stand up to a ghost? *Lulu and Aunt Jerry are useless,* she thought. *Not to mention Ms. Tipton!*

I've got to stop the haunting of Rose Cottage with no help at all.

One of the bananas in the fruit bowl blinked at her.

Okay, maybe I'll have a little help, Nell thought. But what could she and the Netherbeast possibly do about the angry, red feeling that Rose Cottage was drowning in?

And who was Byron?

✦ ✦ ✦

CHAPTER TWELVE

THE MYSTERY TEAM

"Your cat is weird."

It was the first thing Bucky the neighbor boy had said to Nell all morning. They'd been painting Rose Cottage's front door as the loudspeaker in the yard squawked out fake birdsong and terrible soft rock instrumentals.

Nell looked over at Bucky, paintbrush dripping pastel pink onto the newspapers underneath the door. Oh, *great,* what was the Netherbeast doing *now?*

But the black cat was simply rubbing his jowls against the porch railing. "Oh," Nell said, relieved. "That's just regular cat stuff. He's marking his territory with his scent glands."

Bucky dipped his paintbrush, watching the cat weaving in and out of the rail supports. "I thought they peed on stuff to mark territory."

"Mow," went the Netherbeast, lifting his back leg.

"Don't give him any ideas," Nell said.

Bucky shrugged. The front door looked a lot more cheerful with its fresh new color. Nell stepped back to admire it. The Netherbeast decided to rub his face against the wet paint.

"Hey!" Nell snapped. "No!" The Netherbeast lolled his eyes defiantly and kept rubbing. His body got longer and *longer* as he smeared fresh pink paint all across his wormlike torso. The paint rubbed off the door as the Netherbeast squished along, leaving a bare streak across the wood. Then the black-and-pink cat plopped down on the porch floor, paint-side downward.

"Ugh! You are *impossible!*" Nell grunted and reached for her brush. As she slapped more color across the bottom of the door, she heard a sound, ragged and husky, like a goat with laryngitis.

Bucky was laughing. He covered his mouth when Nell looked at him.

Nell felt her face heating up. She spun around. "Look—" she started. She wanted to tell Bucky the

Netherbeast's antics weren't her fault. That it would be easier to get the sky to stop raining by swatting at it with a newspaper! But she couldn't think of how to say it. For a moment, the only sound was the *thuck-thuck-thuck* of Bucky's dad hammering shingles on the roof.

"Fffft!" Nell hissed.

"FffFFFFFfft!" the Netherbeast hissed, mimicking.

"Ha ha, he's the weirdest cat ever!" Bucky laughed. "Weirder than our old cat Mr. Fronjay, who was always licking bags! Your cat is awesome!"

Nell almost dropped her paintbrush. "Really?" She cast a sideways glance at the Netherbeast, who was now licking himself clean. Everywhere tongue touched fur, sizzling vapor rose into the air.

The Netherbeast *was* pretty awesome. When he wasn't being totally annoying.

With a creak, Bucky sat down on the step. "I miss Mr. Fronjay. Now my dad has a chihuahua named Chumbles. He shakes a lot. And he has to wear little sweaters because he gets cold. Chumbles, not my dad."

Nell sat down next to him. "I wonder what the Netherbeast would look like in a little sweater."

The black cat paused mid-lick and glared at Nell. His eyes flared red.

"The Netherbeast?" Bucky raised an eyebrow. "That's his name?"

Nell gulped. Had she said that out loud? "Uh, yeah. After . . . my favorite comic book character." The truth was she didn't know *how* she knew the Netherbeast's name. She definitely hadn't thought of it on her own. "I'm not supposed to have pets," she said, changing the subject just in case Bucky was thinking of asking to borrow her imaginary Netherbeast comic books. "But my parents don't know yet."

"What happens if they don't let you keep him?"

Nell watched the cat swipe at a fat squirrel dancing just out of reach. "I don't know," she said. "I feel like we're a team now. Maybe we'll have to go live in the woods."

Bucky nodded. Nell felt a tingle like she wanted to run away. But maybe it wasn't time yet.

"If you're a team," Bucky said, "what do you do?"

"Huh?"

"Teams *do* things."

Nell thought. Back home in Cape Green, the Netherbeast's strange abilities might have helped her find lost pets, but what about here in Deer Valley? She thought about Rose Cottage and the Flying Florentines. She thought about Lulu's closed eyes and Aunt Jerry's terrified ones. She thought about the voice in the basement—and time running out.

"Maybe we solve mysteries," she said, her heart beating faster as the words came out.

Bucky's eyes widened. "Cool!" He paused, biting his lip. Then he said, "Can I help?"

Nell swallowed. What was she supposed to do now, *tell* him about the spooky voice, about the red feeling in the bones of this house? Was that secretly why she said the word "mysteries" in the first place?

Did she *want* to tell him?

No, she thought. *Don't be weird! This is where I always go wrong trying to make friends.*

Just then, the Netherbeast clomped over, stomping over Nell's crossed legs and dragging his tail across her nose. She jerked her head back before he could rub his butt over her face. But the cat didn't settle in her lap. Instead, he hopped into Bucky's lap and began to knead.

Nell expected Bucky to jump up in alarm, especially as claws began to pick at his overalls. But he just scritched along the black cat's bumpy spine. The Netherbeast curled into a greasy ball, purring disturbingly.

Nell was astonished. The Netherbeast . . . *liked* Bucky.

"Okay," Nell said. "You can help." The cat flashed her an approving glance.

Bucky smiled. "Great! What's our first case?"

Nell took a deep breath. "Obviously, this house."

"Obviously."

"Listen," Nell said in a low voice, "Aunt Jerry hasn't told anybody, but Ms. Tipton's going to close us down if we don't get a five-star review from the Florentines."

Bucky whistled between his teeth. "Wow. That's going to be tough."

"Right. And have you noticed . . ." Nell started, not quite sure how to put it. She tilted her head. "Have you noticed anything *strange* about this house?"

"Like the fact that it's haunted?" Bucky asked.

Nell threw up her hands with relief. "Yes! It's totally haunted, right?"

"*Totally* haunted." Bucky nodded. "And not

with friendly spirits who hide the spoons and stuff. There's something *bad* here."

"*Right?*" Nell leaned toward him. "But the thing is, it wasn't haunted before. The last time I was here, it was just a regular bed and breakfast. Something has changed."

Bucky nodded. "I tried to tell my dad, but he didn't believe me. Not even when he started getting attacked."

Nell gaped at him. "*Attacked?*"

"Yep," Bucky went on. "Last Thursday, the ladder fell over all by itself and stranded him on the roof for three hours. Two days ago, a hammer dropped from a high shelf he didn't remember putting it on and almost cracked his bean." He shivered. "Something here is pretty gosh darned . . ." He lowered his voice to a whisper. "*Ticked off.*"

Nell nodded. "It exploded a light bulb at me this morning . . . I think it's in the basement."

Bucky raised an eyebrow. "The basement?"

Nell inhaled. "There was a voice. In my ear. Nobody there, but this *voice*. A whisper in my head." She glanced back at the house as though it might be listening with gable ears. "So I think we should start there. The basement."

Bucky's eyes widened. "You mean investigate?"

Nell nodded, even though her skin was sprouting goosebumps all over.

"The basement?" Bucky whispered.

CRACK! Suddenly, one of the porch's roof supports snapped in half. The whole heavy beam came smashing down right smack between Nell and Bucky.

"WHOO!" the Netherbeast howled, rocketing away across the lawn.

Nell and Bucky stared at each other.

"Yes," Nell honked, even though every molecule in her body was screaming *NO!* "We definitely need to investigate the basement."

✦ ✦ ✦

CHAPTER THIRTEEN
THE RUMPUS ROOM

Lulu's yellow car had been gone all morning. She and Aunt Jerry had gone to the bridal shop in town to get a new book to use for guests to sign in. The old one was cute and had puppies on it, but Ms. Tipton made Aunt Jerry put it away in a cupboard. According to Ms. Tipton, it was against Sisterhood regulations. Apparently the walls of your B&B could be infested with demons and launching glass shards and hammers at your head so long as you had a guest book that followed the rules.

That was fine with Nell. She and Bucky were going to check out the basement, and Nell wanted an exactly zero percent chance that Lulu would trap her down there again.

Nell hadn't had a friend in a long time. Well, other than the animals at the shelter. When she was younger, Nell had had a few school friends.

Lena invited Nell to her birthday party. Saad and his mom showed her how to bake cookies after school. But Nell always seemed to be thinking about something else, anxious for the next thing. And, all right, she used to talk about the animals at the shelter quite a bit.

Okay, a *lot*.

The other kids thought it was interesting at first, but eventually Nell went from *interesting* to *irritating* to—

Weird.

Then she got a huge zit and the rumor started that she had caught the bubonic plague from her secret army of rats. That was a fun spring. She stopped talking in school so much after that. Then she just kind of forgot how. But now . . .

"What's down there?" Bucky whispered as they stood at door to the basement steps.

"I don't know," Nell said. "Musty smells."

"RrrrRRR!" The Netherbeast put his nose to the crack under the door and began to growl. A cold draft swirled around their feet, creeping like ice through the holes in Nell's sneakers. She gulped. Going back into the basement had seemed like a reasonable plan outside in the sunshine. Now it seemed completely cuckoo.

She swung the door open. Nell expected the Netherbeast to hightail it back outside as soon as she opened the door. But instead, he sprinted down the wooden steps into the gloom. "Okay, turn on the flashlight."

Bucky patted his pockets. "I lost it!"

"You set it down on the little table with the curly legs," Nell said. "The one with the dead plant on it."

Bucky hopped across the hall. "Wow, how'd you remember that?"

"I'm very observant." *That was kind of an obnoxious thing to say,* Nell thought. But reuniting people with what they had lost was one of her few talents she was proud of, so it had come out that way.

Bucky switched on the plastic flashlight and they peered down the stairs. Not a sound came from below. The cold updraft touched their faces and billowed inside the sleeves of their T-shirts.

"Okay," Nell said. "Well." She meant to say, *Let's go.* But the words didn't come out. *You've got to help Aunt Jerry and Rose Cottage,* she told herself. An evil basement was definitely bad for business.

With a deep breath, Nell stepped into the shadows. Bucky followed, the beam of his light swinging from side to side, illuminating unfinished wood, concrete, and cobwebs.

Suddenly, a pair of glowing, red eyes sparked the darkness.

Nell and Bucky yelped. The flashlight went clattering down the stairs.

The Netherbeast sauntered out of the gloom, his eyes like scarlet laser beams. Nell breathed a sigh of relief.

Bucky did not. "Your *cat!*" he whimpered. "He has *red flashlight eyes?*" He turned to scamper back up the stairs, but Nell put a hand on his arm.

"Wait!" she said. "I can explain!"

Bucky looked at her with wide eyes. ". . . And?"

Nell looked down at the Netherbeast, then back up at Bucky. "Yes. Well, it's very simple." She swallowed. "My cat, who *is* a cat, sometimes, uh . . ." Her voice trailed off. She didn't know what to say.

Bucky raised his eyebrows. "Sometimes what?" he whispered. Below, two red beams made their way around the edges of the basement. Every once in a while they'd flicker when the Netherbeast blinked.

"My cat sometimes . . ." Nell started. She let go of Bucky's arm. It was no use. "Sometimes . . . has red flashlight eyes. Or turns into a puddle. Or makes the sky go black. Even though he's supposed to *be normal*," she yelled meaningfully down the stairs. Then she turned back to Bucky. "He has a hard time being normal. He forgets. Or something."

Bucky just stared at her.

This is the moment, Nell realized. Bucky would run away and never look back. She knew from experience, when she told a story that was one story too many, or laughed a laugh that was one honk too loud, or made a remark that was one banana too strange. She knew the look, the one that meant, *It's over.* And now, on top of everything else, there was the Netherbeast, who was too many, too loud, and too banana all at once.

But Bucky didn't run. He looked at the Netherbeast, then at Nell. Then he shrugged and said, "Okay."

Nell blinked. Was that it? *Okay?*

She gave him a weak smile. "Oh. Okay."

Nell turned back to the basement, which suddenly didn't seem quite as frightening anymore. There was a light switch at the bottom of the stairs, and in an instant they were blinking in the dusty glow of a round overhead lamp.

"I don't know what I expected," Nell murmured.

"But it wasn't this," Bucky finished for her.

They stared around the basement. Instead of the monster-infested dungeon that Nell had imagined, there was an old orange shag carpet, ugly flowered wallpaper, shelves of musty books and board games, a foosball table, a squat television with knobs, and a rust-colored sofa.

"It's just a room," Nell said.

A grin spread across Bucky's face. "It's a rumpus room!" He slid a game from a shelf and blew the dust off it. *"Risk."* He gave the box a gentle shake, rattling a collection of little somethings inside. "My mom and I used to play this."

Nell ran her fingers over the handles of the foosball table. "Where's the ball? Maybe—" But she stopped short when she saw the Netherbeast.

He was standing in front of the sofa. His claws clutched the carpet and his back arched so high he might as well have been a grimy black rainbow. His red laser beam eyes were focused on—

On something in front of him.

Something on the couch.

Someone—

sitting on the couch.

And glowing.

✦ ✦ ✦

CHAPTER FOURTEEN
THE GHOST

Nell gasped. There, on the couch in the rumpus room, was a shape: the faint, glowing outline of legs, a lap, a torso, shoulders, and wisps of luminous hair clinging to a round head. The face had deep wrinkles and a scowling mouth. And the eyes—the terrible eyes were the clearest part, sparkling in the murky basement light.

It was an old man. *Only he isn't real,* Nell thought. *He isn't really here . . . Is he?*

The Netherbeast could certainly see him. And wasn't happy about it.

Bucky's back was to the couch as he rummaged through the shelves, but Nell couldn't find her voice to alert him.

"MROWWWW!" the Netherbeast yowled like a fire engine being tortured.

Bucky jumped. "Son of a biscuit!"

The gleaming eyes on the sofa swiveled in his direction. Bucky looked at Nell, unnerved. "What ails that cat? Why did he screech?"

Nell felt electric tingles going all up and down her legs and arms, running over her scalp and ears. She pointed at the thing on the rust-colored sofa.

It was a ghost. *The* ghost. It had to be.

And it looked just like the man in the portrait upstairs in the hall.

Bucky followed Nell's finger and squinted. "What?" he asked.

Nell stared at the translucent man. "You don't see him?" she whispered.

Bucky asked, carefully, "See who?" Then he shut his eyes tight and muttered, "Don't say a ghost, don't say a ghost, don't say a ghost . . ."

"Uh," Nell began. ". . . A specter?"

Bucky whimpered and slunk behind the foosball table, as though the little plastic soccer players could protect him.

"You really don't see him?" Nell asked.

Bucky shook his head. His frightened eyes darted around the room. "What's he doing?" he whispered.

"He's just sitting there," Nell said. *Whose shaky, scaredy-moose voice is that?* she wondered. *Oh, nuts, it's mine.*

The Netherbeast was now so fluffed out he was spherical. He rolled back and forth over the orange shag carpet like the world's angriest pom-pom, spitting and hissing, his eyes shooting sparks from their corners. The ghost of the old man turned toward him and glared. The black pom-pom started to swell aggressively.

"Hey!" Nell managed to bark, snapping her fingers at the Netherbeast. "Don't antagonize the specter!" With a grumble, the black pom-pom deflated and rolled underneath the foosball table, causing Bucky to take a nervous step back.

That got the old man's attention. He turned his spectral gaze on Nell.

"What's he doing now?" Bucky asked, looking all around the room.

"He's—" Nell started. "He's *getting up*." She planted her feet. The ghost took a wobbly step toward her. Nell gasped. The ghost took another jerky step in her direction. "He's coming toward me," she murmured.

"Talk to him," Bucky squeaked. Easy for him to say.

How do you talk to a ghost? Nell wondered. Dogs and cats were easy. They carried their emotions on their outsides. But this glowering old man with his glittering eyes—all Nell could feel was the heavy, red feeling. Rose Cottage was submerged in it. Was this man's anger filling the entire house?

The ghost stopped inches from her face. Cold breath swirled from him; not just from his scowling mouth, but his glowing paper face and wispy hair. Nell planted her feet. Her skeleton felt like it wanted to burst right through her skin and start running.

"*He's . . . right . . . here,*" she murmured. Bucky covered his eyes. The Netherbeast skittered up onto the foosball table and started clawing at the rods, spinning all the plastic players at once into twenty-two colorful blurs.

The old man was so close, Nell could see all the way through his gleaming head. The room behind him rippled like it was underwater. Nell took a deep breath. "Hello?" she said tentatively. "Mr. . . . Ghost?"

Suddenly, the cracked, luminous lips started to move. An icy breeze snaked its way over Nell's face and into her ears.

"Sorry, I didn't catch that." Nell leaned in, one ear tilted forward. "What?" she whispered.

"*BYRON!*" The old man's voice exploded, reverberating around the rumpus room, shaking the shelves, rattling game pieces in their faded boxes.

With a screech, Nell, Bucky, and the Netherbeast sprinted back up the basement stairs, slamming the door behind them.

✦ ✦ ✦

CHAPTER FIFTEEN

A VISIT TO TOWN HALL

Bucky strode down the only sidewalk in Deer Valley, which edged its quarter-mile stretch of sleepy downtown. He walked quickly, like he was confident, but Nell knew they were both still jumpy from being shouted at by a ghost. Well, Bucky hadn't heard the old man's voice, but he had definitely noticed the shockwave that had rattled everything in the rumpus room—and it clearly wasn't just a random earthquake. It was a ghostquake.

Nell trotted along beside him, the Netherbeast fragrantly draped across her bony shoulders. If Nell were a moose, the Netherbeast was her pelt after she'd been swimming in a bog.

"Do you know anything about the people who used to live at Rose Cottage?" she asked.

"Yeah," Bucky said, a little out of breath. "Old Mr. Eslick." He lowered his voice. "He was a mean son-of-a-biscuit, as my dad says."

"That *must* be him in the rumpus room. And his portrait in the hall," Nell said. "Once we know who 'Byron' is, we'll be a step closer to finding out why this . . ." She still didn't want to say *ghost*. "Why this guy is so angry."

"I don't see why we can't just ask your aunt," Bucky said.

"She already thinks I'm weird," Nell said. "And Ms. Tipton will flip her shoes if anybody even hints at something supernatural going on. We have to figure this out on our own."

They were headed to the Deer Valley town hall. As they crested a lump of a hill, Bucky pointed to a white clapboard building just ahead. "Here we are. If anyone can help us figure out who Byron is, Mrs. Desjardins can. She knows everything about everybody."

They scurried up the steps. The town hall had metal doors with push bars on the back. The Netherbeast dropped to the floor like an earthquake and raced off down a hallway before Nell had a chance to get both feet inside.

There was a window in the wall labeled TOWN CLERK. The counter looked onto a cluttered office where a khaki-covered derriere was sticking out from between two file cabinets. A sign pointed down the hallway: SELECTMEN, CEMETERY TRUSTEE, and RESTROOM.

Bucky reached a wave across the counter. "Hi, Mrs. Desjardins!"

"Oh, hello, Bucky." A short woman popped out from between the file cabinets. She was carrying a stack of license plates. "One second." Mrs. Desjardins clattered the plates onto a desk, then scuttled over to the window. "Who's your friend?" Her enormous glasses made her eyes look tiny.

"This is Nell," Bucky said, as Nell felt her face heat up with self-consciousness. "She's Ms. Moufflon's niece."

"Oh!" Mrs. Desjardins leaned forward. "How's it going up at Rose Cottage, dear?"

"Great," Nell said. *Great. Yeah.*

Mrs. Desjardins straightened up and gave an approving smile-nod. "That's nice to hear. Seems like all I hear are wackadoo rumors about that place!"

Nell gulped.

Mrs. Desjardins asked, "Now, what can I do for you?"

"What was old Mr. Eslick's first name?" Bucky asked. "The man who used to live there, before Ms. Moufflon?"

Nell expected the town clerk to begin a new shuffle through the file cabinets, but instead she just screwed up her face and thought.

"Gord, wasn't it?" Mrs. Desjardins said. "Gordon? Yes, I'm sure that was it. Gordon Eslick. Only saw him once a year, when he would come down here and put up the most awful stink about registering that old rattletrap car of his."

"His name wasn't Byron?" Nell asked.

Mrs. Desjardins frowned. "Byron? Nope. Can't say I know any Byrons, to be honest. There was a Lord Byron, wasn't there? Don't think he lived around here, though."

"It sounds like kind of an old name," Bucky said. "Mrs. Desjardins, do you know who lived in Rose Cottage *before* Mr. Eslick?"

"Before?" Mrs. Desjardins squinted her tiny eyes, trying to call forth the information from the filing cabinet in her brain. "No idea, dear. Whoever it was was gone when I got here. Always been old Mr. Eslick—well, ever since his kids moved out."

"Kids?" An idea sparked in Nell's mind. "Did he have a son named Byron?"

Mrs. Desjardins tapped a fingernail on the counter. "He did have a son. Played the trumpet in the school band with my girl Delores. What was his name? Skeet? Sploot? Scoot. Scoot Eslick." The town clerk nodded. "He scooted out of there as quick as a wink once he turned eighteen, I'll tell you. That boy wasn't going to hang around. He still comes back to Deer Valley from time to time, but never spoke to his dad again, that's what they say. The wife, she'd left before that." She leaned forward. "Not to speak ill, but—well, Mr. Eslick was a *difficult man.*" Mrs. Desjardins blinked, adding to nobody in particular, "One wonders if that man was ever happy at all. *Sweet flapping jackrabbits!*"

Nell jumped as an ear-piercing wail filled the hall. Mrs. Desjardins's mouth dropped open. She pointed at something behind Nell and Bucky, her eyes as round as little white peas.

Nell spun around. With a *thump,* the Netherbeast launched himself at the metal doors. There he clung, spread like a cat tapestry across the width of the doorway. His fur was soaking wet. Water polluted with fur-yuck ran in dark rivulets down the doors and pooled on the floor. It was an altogether frightening spectacle.

Nell felt the blood drain from her face. "My, uh, cat wants to go out."

Mrs. Desjardins made a gurgling sound.

"Sorry, it must be an emergency!" Bucky blurted as he and Nell sprinted to the doorway. "He gets the poops sometimes! Thanks for your help!"

Nell pried the sopping cat's claws away from the doorframe. The Netherbeast continued to howl. Nell had no idea what he had done, but it wasn't a good idea to hang around and find out.

There was the sound of a distant flush, then the slam of a door, followed by rushed footsteps thwapping toward them down the hall. "Was that a *cat?*"

"Gotta go," Bucky yelled. They threw open the doors and sprinted outside.

✦ ✦ ✦

CHAPTER SIXTEEN
GROWN-UPS

It was late afternoon as Nell and Bucky made their way back to Rose Cottage. The wind had picked up, and the Netherbeast glided along as though he were on invisible roller skates, weaving in and out of their legs. Nell tripped over him and tumbled forward onto the sidewalk.

"Cats don't glide!" Nell managed to snap as she fell, *thud.* The Netherbeast gave a hissy little sniff. He trotted away, doing a high step with his paws. Nell clambered to her feet again, all knobby moose limbs. "Be a *cat!*" she called.

"Sorry Mrs. Desjardins couldn't help us," Bucky said as they turned into Rose Cottage's driveway. Bucky's dad's white van was still parked outside, and Lulu's yellow albatross of a car had returned as well. Luckily, there was no sign of Ms. Tipton's shiny car.

The Netherbeast leaped onto Lulu's roof and bounded from there to the top of the porch, where he sat surveying the estate.

"She did help a little," Nell said, "because now, at least, we know Old Man Eslick isn't Byron."

"Glad to see you two getting along," came a deep voice. A man stood in the driveway, looking dusty and sweaty. He wore a faded T-shirt and jeans and had the same nose as Bucky.

"Dad, this is Nell," Bucky said.

The man held out his hand and Nell shook it. "Nice to meet you, Mr. Denver," she said. Or tried to. It came out as a whisper. Bucky raised one eyebrow. Nell wanted to crawl into a hole.

But Mr. Denver just smiled and said, "Charmed." He leaned against the van and took a swig from a water bottle that said *Deer Valley Savings Bank* up the side. "So where were you guys this afternoon?"

"Sorry, Dad," Bucky said. "We finished painting the door and had some business at town hall."

Mr. Denver raised his eyebrows. "Business at town hall, eh? Don't tell me you've gone and registered a new speedboat I don't know about." He took another swig. "On second thought, *do* tell me that. A new speedboat would be awesome!"

"We were trying to find out more about the people who used to live in this house," Nell said.

"You mean Old Man Eslick?" Mr. Denver shook his head. "Nell, don't let this little scamp scare you with his spooky stories." He raised an eyebrow at Bucky. "There's no such thing as ghosts. Trust me, I've poked around in a lot of old houses. Nothing but dusty furniture and trunks full of bric-a-brac. Sometimes a dead mouse."

At that moment, a gust of wind howled through the scaffolding against the wall. A brick flew off the roof and hurled itself *smack* at Mr. Denver's head.

"Woo!" Mr. Denver ducked as the brick sailed by at a hundred miles an hour. He went back to leaning on the van, completely unbothered.

Nell's jaw dropped. Bucky pointed an accusing finger and said, *"See?"*

Mr. Denver laughed. "Oh, these old houses! Always creaking and squeaking and throwing their bricks around." He tapped the door of the van. "Time to head out, Starbuck. There's a pizza in the freezer with our name on it."

Bucky gave a frustrated sigh. "Bye, Nell," he said. "See you tomorrow?"

Nell nodded. Bucky and his dad pulled out of the driveway and the van disappeared around the corner.

Nell made her way back up Rose Cottage's front steps. Her stomach was doing flip-flops. The flips were tingly and warm. They were thoughts of a new friend who wanted to see her tomorrow. The flops were sickening and cold. They were the idea that not a single grown-up was going to believe her and Bucky about the ghost in the basement and the angry feeling that filled the rooms and halls of the bed and breakfast. Not even Lulu, who wasn't a grown-up, but might have been able to help if she'd only listened. It figured. Lulu never helped when it was important.

CHAPTER SEVENTEEN
THE NETHERBEAST DESTROYS
A BEANBAG CHAIR

Nell and Bucky followed Aunt Jerry down the wooden stairs to the rumpus room. *Clack-clack-clack* went Aunt Jerry's chunky heels. *Fwop-fwop-fwop* went Nell's and Bucky's sneakers. *Clickety-clickety-clicky-click-click-clickety-click* went all the Netherbeast's extra claws he had been wearing lately.

"Well, let's get to work on this dusty old basement, shall we?" Aunt Jerry said.

Nell half-expected the ghost of Mr. Eslick to have been a dream. There couldn't *still* be a glowing old man with glittering eyes sitting on the sofa, could there?

But as they all bustled into the rumpus room with their brooms and dustrags, there he was. Still sitting, still glowing, and still scowling just like in his portrait upstairs.

"Byron!" the ghost grumbled. A pile of books came crashing down off a side table. Everybody jumped.

Nell yelped. She looked at Bucky and Aunt Jerry. They had jumped at the crashing books, but they didn't seem to notice anything else out of the ordinary. Like, for instance, the ghost on the couch staring at Nell with a sour-apple frown.

Nell stared back at him. And the more she stared, the more she realized that she really wasn't afraid of him anymore. True, it had been *shocking* to encounter a gleaming specter from beyond the grave. But this old man wasn't actually that *scary*.

He seemed like . . . just a grumpy old man.

Who happened to be dead.

And who also happened to be able to knock books around and hurl bricks at people's heads. That definitely wouldn't fly with the Florentines.

Aunt Jerry surveyed the room with her hands on her hips. "You were absolutely right, Nelly. This place could use a little sprucing up. Dust everywhere, books falling over. My goodness." She looked at Nell. "I'm glad you brought it up. You know, I started in here a while ago, when Ms. Tipton first arrived. She said it was an eyesore. Got rid of a few ratty old things. But when everything started going wrong, I kind of lost track." She sighed. "It's hard to care about an outdated basement nobody sees when upstairs all the rugs are unraveling and the portraits are crying."

Nell blinked. "The *portraits* were *crying?*"

"We should organize these games," Bucky said, pulling boxes off a shelf.

The translucent old man on the couch glared at them. "Byron!" he snapped.

"Yeah, Byron," Nell mumbled to him. "I get it, okay?" Only she didn't get it. Not at all.

The old man squinted, irritated, and crossed his arms.

Nell started to gather the books that had tumbled onto the orange carpet, stacking them on the side table.

"Byron!" the ghost snapped, making the stack of books fall over again.

Nell did her best to ignore him. She scooped up the books. This time, after she'd finished tidying them into a pile, it was the Netherbeast who knocked them over. The ghost laughed nastily.

"Ugh!" Nell grunted. "You!" she hissed at the Netherbeast. "Behave like a cat! Cats don't—" She stopped herself. Knocking books over after someone had just stacked them was *exactly* what cats did.

The Netherbeast plummeted onto the carpet and began sniffing a lumpy brown beanbag chair that had been shoved into the corner next to the television. After a few good sniffs, all the fur on his fluffy black tail stood out straight. "Mow!"

"What is it?" Nell put her hands on her hips. "Something else you want to ruin?"

Apparently the answer was *yes*, because all of a sudden the Netherbeast began attacking the beanbag chair like a tornado.

"Hey!" Nell said, trying to pull the soft vinyl furniture away from the furious cat.

Aunt Jerry let out a squeak. "What's wrong with your cat? Is it rabid?"

"No," Nell said, trying to wrestle the beanbag chair from the angry black blur. "Well . . . maybe."

With a grunt, she wrenched the beanbag chair free. It *rrrripped* in two. Beans exploded across the rumpus room like a snowstorm. Every surface was covered.

For a moment, nobody moved. Then Aunt Jerry said, in a small voice, "I'll go get the vacuum." She clonked up the stairs on her chunky heels.

Bucky stared at the Netherbeast. "What did you *do?*" He started to brush beans into a wastebasket. The Netherbeast bounced over to the remains of the beanbag chair and kept clawing.

Bucky glanced behind him to make sure Aunt Jerry was gone. "Is the ghost, you know . . . *here?*"

Nell nodded. "Yep. And he's annoying." She flopped down onto the rust-colored sofa.

"Byron!" the ghost next to her said testily.

"All right!" Nell snapped. "Byron! Who is Byron?"

The ghost of Mr. Eslick gave her an offended look, but didn't say anything else.

"Hey." Bucky was standing over the beanbag chair. "What's this?" Nell went over to see what he was looking at.

"Rrrr!" The Netherbeast lashed his tail.

Nell bent down. She was surprised to find something crumpled up inside the folds of brown vinyl. "There's something here," she said. "A hidden message?"

"Maybe the Netherbeast was trying to help us out after all," Bucky said.

"Mew." The Netherbeast sat back on his haunches with an air of superiority.

Nell unfolded the crumpled thing. "It's an old photograph! It must have gotten stuck in the seam."

"Let's take a look!" Bucky craned his neck over her shoulder. "It's a picture of—*here.*"

Sure enough, the black and white photo had clearly been taken in the back garden of Rose Cottage. There was the screenhouse, the beds of flowers looking much less wild, the clapboards with unflaking paint. And in the foreground, posing unhappily for a portrait, was a young boy. His hair had been slicked down, his shoes were polished, and his shorts had been ironed. In his arms, he clutched a well-worn teddy bear.

"It's this house, but who is that boy?" Bucky wondered aloud.

"Byron!" the ghost said. His eyes were glowing white eggs.

Nell flipped the photo over. On the back, a name had been written in curving pencil. She looked at Bucky in surprise. "He's right. It's Byron."

CHAPTER EIGHTEEN
THE BOY IN THE PICTURE

There were no more photos in the beanbag chair. And no more beans, either—they were all over the rumpus room, between the sofa cushions, balanced on the heads of the plastic foosball players, even nestled in Nell's hair. After the Netherbeast's fit of destruction, Ms. Tipton and Aunt Jerry decided the easiest way to deal with the mess was just to close the door and pretend the whole basement didn't exist.

For the next two weeks, everyone worked hard to get Rose Cottage in shape for the arrival of the famous Flying Florentines. The town building inspector, Mrs. Fennel, went over every inch of the B&B, writing things on a clipboard and shaking her head. Nell and Bucky planted flowers, vacuumed, washed windows, and put clean sheets on the beds. Aunt Jerry stocked the kitchen with delicious breakfast foods. Lulu feng shui'ed the bedrooms and worked with the electrician to fix all the wonky wiring and broken lights. Mr. Denver repaired the roof, replaced the rotten windowsills, and carted away the remains of the old back porch. And Ms. Tipton sipped tea and made sure everyone was following the Cozy Corners Sisterhood of Inns, LLC's long and detailed list of rules. One afternoon, she made Nell get rid of an entire case of specially made Rose Cottage pencils because they were the wrong shape. Nell had no idea how a pencil could be the wrong shape, but at least the Deer Valley Rec Center was happy with the donation.

Rose Cottage was looking better, Nell thought as she and the Netherbeast sat under a rosebush in the garden. It was starting to look like its old self. Good thing, too—the Florentines would be there in only two days.

But the truth was none of their hard work would matter if the ghost of Old Man Eslick decided to throw a tantrum. What if he shivered all the shingles off the roof again? Or popped the pipes loose from the toilets? Or decided to start hurling dangerous objects at the Florentines' photogenic faces? All Rose Cottage's chances of a five-star review, any shot Nell had at getting Ms. Tipton's glowing reference, Lulu's precious summer job—all of it would evaporate like a slushie in a bonfire.

But how to get rid of Old Man Eslick? Or at least cheer him up? Nell had thought the photograph of the mystery boy they'd discovered was the key. But so far, it wasn't helping after all.

"No idea," Aunt Jerry said, turning the picture over in her sparkly-nailed fingers. "Where did you get this? It says 'Byron' on the back. I had a teacher named Miss Byron when I was in elementary school. She looked like one of those beaky songbirds. She had this inner ear condition that made her fall over a lot. Like a little bird falling over with its legs in the air, *fweep!* It was quite sad."

Bucky's dad was equally unhelpful. "Hm. Byron? Doesn't look familiar," he said. "Have you tried the Internet?"

Bucky put up flyers around town with copies of the photograph and *DO YOU KNOW WHO I AM?* printed in big letters across the bottom. Lulu said the local teenagers thought it was some kind of viral marketing thing.

Only the ancient town librarian, Mr. Beaufort, gave them a glimmer of hope. He stared at the photograph for a long time before saying, "This boy looks so familiar . . ." Nell and Bucky waited, holding their breath. But Mr. Beaufort, after squinting and pursing his lips and clicking his tongue, finally just shook his head and said, "Nope. Sorry. He must just look like someone I know."

Now, as Nell sat under the rosebush on a perfectly nice, sunny morning, frustration gnawed at her. She realized that, underneath all Rose Cottage's problems, there was something special about the B&B. It wasn't just the funny, fancy little rooms with lace doilies and scrolly woodwork. Maybe it was all the affection Aunt Jerry had poured into it over the years—her hands running a dustcloth over the banister, carefully cleaning the old window glass with newspapers and vinegar, trimming the rosebushes and straightening the birdfeeders. That sort of care must leave a mark on the spirit of a place, right? Maybe those echoes could be more powerful than a ghost's hissy fits.

The world seemed more confusing than ever. But as Nell looked at the Netherbeast, who was purring like a chainsaw while gnawing on a rose branch, she felt he was less confusing than everything else. At least the Netherbeast knew what he was doing. Always. Even if it was something horrible, the Netherbeast *meant* to be doing it, and to be doing it exactly that way.

"What would you do if the meanest girl in school called you a moose?" Nell asked the cat.

The Netherbeast thoughtfully chewed a mouthful of thorns.

"What if you were sent away from the only place where you didn't feel like a moose?" Nell closed her eyes. "What if the only person who ever made you feel less . . . moosey . . . became a different person? And suddenly all they cared about was *leaving* you and going away to stupid college?"

The Netherbeast spat out the rose branch. He flipped onto his back and waggled his paws. Nell smiled and rubbed his fluffy tum.

The Netherbeast chomped her fingers.

"Ow!" Nell jerked her hand back in pain. Then she laughed. *"You'll* never change. You'll always be

as *yourself* as you can be. I'm pretty sure of that."
She sat back. "And you know? I think that's a good
thing." She closed her eyes. "I'm going to need a
Band-Aid."

✦ ✦ ✦

CHAPTER NINETEEN
THE MAN AT THE
COFFEE SHOP

"**C**ats are not allowed in this coffee shop," Nell muttered to the thing draped around her shoulders.

"Actually, cats *are* allowed in this coffee shop!" said the perky barista.

You're not helping was what Nell wanted to say. Instead, she whispered a *thank you* and slid her mint-chocolate latte off the counter. She found a table in the corner and set up her laptop. A couple of pleasant coffeeshop cats padded over to investigate, but scampered away again when they got a glimpse, or maybe a whiff, of the Netherbeast.

"Stay out of my video call," Nell said to the Netherbeast. He gave a hoarse chirp of protest. Then he stretched. He curled himself all the way around Nell's neck, his bones dissolving, until he was nothing more than a long, furry, boneless abomination. With a pink tongue.

Nell rolled her eyes. "What are you supposed to be, a *scarf?*"

The tongue went *flp-flp-flp.*

"No. *No,*" Nell said. "You can't disguise yourself as a scarf. Why would I wear a scarf in the middle of summer? Especially one that looks like I unearthed it from somebody's grave in the dead of night?"

A teenage boy on his way to the café's bathroom gave Nell a strange look. She cleared her throat and pretended to be fascinated by her desktop. When he was gone, she dug her fingers under the squishy fur tube around her neck and slid it off onto the table. "Just sit there," she told it. "Just be a *cat* sitting there—behind my laptop, until the call is over. Don't be wei—don't be distracting. Mom and Barb are not ready for you. The last thing I need is them hopping in the car to come check on me."

Nell had tried not to think too much about the end of summer. When she'd first discovered the Netherbeast in Lulu's car, the weeks ahead seemed endless. *Of course* she could figure something out. But the days were slipping by, and she still had no idea what she was going to tell her parents about the stray cat who'd adopted her.

As Nell waited for Mom and Barb to call at the scheduled time, she investigated. *Byron Deer Valley,* she searched. *Gordon Eslick Byron.* What was the mystery? Maybe someone's bones weren't resting easy. Maybe there had been a crime. *Byron death. Byron murder. Missing Byron.* Nothing. The web was about as helpful as the Netherbeast, who was busy licking the varnish off the tabletop.

Getting rid of ghosts, she searched. The Internet had a lot of opinions about this. Rituals, herbs, priests, spells. Most of these things would be hard to do without Ms. Tipton noticing, especially the suggestion about burning the house to the ground and starting over from scratch. One thing everyone who claimed to know about this stuff seemed to agree on, though, was that ghosts were here for a reason. Something was unfinished. *Unresolved suffering.*

Beep! Beep! Nell's thoughts were interrupted by the incoming video call—noon on the dot.

Before she answered, she pointed a stern finger at the black cat perched on the table behind her computer. "Stay out of frame. And behave."

The Netherbeast looked back with wide, innocent eyes, as if to say, *Who, me?*

Nell took a deep breath and clicked *Answer.* But somehow, in that fraction of a second, the faux Netherbeast scarf was back around her neck. Now it was arranged in a stylish infinite-loop design, and the mangy black fur was speckled with gold glitter.

Before Nell could even gasp, or shriek an inappropriate word in the middle of the coffee shop, her parents' magnified faces popped up on the screen.

"Hi, sweetie!"

"Hi," Nell honked, petrified.

"Well, look at you!" Barb fiddled with her dainty glasses. "Is that a new scarf?"

". . . Yes."

Mom frowned. "Isn't it a bit warm for a scarf?"

". . . Yes."

Barb grinned. "Well, Nell, I can't believe you're going to meet the Flying Florentines! Are you excited?"

"Nobody's more excited than you, Barb," Mom said with a laugh.

"Oh, it's so true! Please remember all the details! I want to know what they're really like." Barb's eyes were glittering with exhilaration. The only thing she loved almost as much as visiting interesting places was hearing about other people visiting interesting places. And the Florentines visited some very interesting places. Not that Deer Valley was one of them.

"How's everything going?" Mom asked.

"Okay." Nell swallowed. There was an awkward silence. Her scarf farted quietly.

"I saw Shana yesterday," Mom said. "She says hi. Wanted you to know things are fine at the shelter."

Fine without me, Nell thought.

"She's looking forward to hearing all about your summer job." Mom got misty-eyed. "So grown up!"

"Yep," Nell said.

"How's Lulu?" Barb asked. "How's that funny old car running?"

"Good," Nell said. She realized she wasn't exactly being a sparkling conversationalist. What would a responsible adult talk about? "Uh, we have a new forsythia. I'm, uh, in charge of dusting it." Nell still didn't know what a forsythia was.

Mom blinked. "Dusting it? That's quite, er—"

But Nell didn't hear the rest of the sentence. Because at that moment, a man passed by her table, heading for the exit. He had graying hair, a crooked nose, and rounded shoulders. He looked about Nell's parents' age.

Even so, she knew immediately who he was. He looked just like the mysterious little boy in the photograph. And he was getting away.

"Hang on," she said into her laptop. "I have to go to the bathroom." As her mom started to say something, she flipped the screen closed and jumped out of her chair. The glitter scarf opened its eyes curiously.

"Sir?" Nell called after the man. Her voice was small and hoarse. She tried again, hurrying through the café and out the door. "Sir . . . s-IR?"

The man ahead of her on the sidewalk didn't turn around. Nell ran to catch up. "Stop him!" she hissed at the Netherbeast.

The Netherbeast leaped into action. He bounded ahead. When he reached the striding man, he cut in front of him and did a classic cat-rub against his shins.

The man's legs hit the Netherbeast like a concrete wall and he tumbled forward, *splat!*, onto the sidewalk. Wallet, keys, phone, tissues, a bottle of antacid tablets, and a granola bar went flying from his pockets in all directions.

"Oh, my gosh!" Nell gasped. "I'm so sorry!"

The man looked up angrily. If he could have shot flame out of his face and burned off Nell's eyebrows then and there, she was pretty sure he would have. He pointed at the Netherbeast. "Is that *your*—"

"I'm *so sorry*," Nell interrupted, "that this awful cat, who I've never seen before in my life, came out of nowhere and tripped you like that!"

The man narrowed his eyes and harrumphed. He got to his feet and began collecting his scattered things.

"Can I help—" Nell started, but the man cut her off.

"Just leave me alone."

"My name is—"

"Leave me alone." The man gave Nell one last dirty look and stomped off down the sidewalk.

Nell watched him go. "Wow. What a grump."

The Netherbeast looked scandalized. Then his attention was caught by something on the ground. Nell saw it, too—small and white, flipping and sliding down the sidewalk in the breeze. She snatched it up. "His business card!"

The back of the card listed a phone number and address in the city. Nell turned the card over.

BYRON "SCOOT" ESLICK

FINE ANTIQUES

BOUGHT & SOLD | RESTORATION

Nell's jaw dropped. She hadn't expected this. *Scoot Eslick. Byron "Scoot" Eslick.* Old Man Eslick's son, the one who moved out—and never spoke to his dad again.

If that wasn't unresolved suffering, Nell didn't know what was.

And now she knew what she had to do.

✦ ✦ ✦

CHAPTER TWENTY

A RARE FIND

"**B**ut I don't know what to say." Bucky stared at his phone. In his other hand, he held Byron "Scoot" Eslick's business card.

Nell snipped a zinnia and added it to her bouquet. Ms. Tipton insisted the Florentines had to have local flowers waiting for them in their room when they arrived. Luckily, the ghost of Old Man Eslick hadn't killed this latest crop. Maybe it was extra healthy due to all the fertilizer the Netherbeast had been distributing.

Behind Nell and Bucky, the parlor window was open and they could hear Lulu and Aunt Jerry doing some last-minute furniture arranging inside. Bucky's dad had finally finished all his projects—until this morning, when the mailbox disintegrated into a pile of dust. Mr. Denver was at the end of the driveway now, driving a new post into the ground.

"Tell him anything you want," Nell said. "Tell him he's won a million dollars. Anything to get him over here. We've got to patch things up between him and Old Man Eslick and resolve all the unresolved suffering. Before the Florentines arrive."

"Why don't *you* tell him?" Bucky said.

"Because I'm not good at talking on the phone," Nell murmured. She snipped another zinnia.

Bucky sighed, then tapped in the number. After a moment, he said into the phone, "Hello. I'm from, uh . . . Rose Cottage Bed and Breakfast."

Nell gave him a thumbs up.

Bucky swallowed. "Uh. We—uh—we have your father in the basement."

Nell shook her head vigorously.

Bucky looked stricken. "Oh. Oh, he is?" Nell could hear an agitated voice at the other end of the line. "Well, I mean, we have *somebody's* father in the basement . . ."

"Ugh!" Nell grabbed the phone. "Hello?"

"Who is this?" Scoot Eslick's tinny voice snapped. "Is this a prank? What do you mean you have my deceased father tied up in the basement?"

"I'm sorry, uh, this is a huge mis-understanding," Nell said quickly. Her voice was cracking all over the place. And she wasn't sure what to say next. "Um."

Then she saw the Netherbeast sitting majestically—yes, *majestically*—on top of a stone garden wall. He was poised and sleek, like an onyx statue carved in tribute to a god. He stared at her with imperturbable golden eyes.

He was . . . glorious.

"Wow," Nell whispered. She imagined the Netherbeast having a phone conversation. There would be no *ums*, no *I'm sorrys*. Everything would be as smooth as onyx.

And somehow, she turned on the most confident, most anti-moose voice there ever was. "Do I have the honor of addressing Mr. Byron Eslick, purveyor of fine antiques?"

There was a pause. "What do you want?"

Purveyor. That was a good word. It seemed to have done the trick. "My associates and I represent the . . . vaulted estate of Rose Cottage Manor, and we have been cataloguing and inventorying its . . . remarkable holdings."

There was another pause. "You what? What is all that gibberish supposed to mean?"

Nell wasn't exactly sure, but she pushed on. "It *means*," she said. "It *means* that we have been going through the antiques in your former childhood home, which is now a bed and breakfast. And—*and*—we have discovered . . ." She paused for effect. "A rare find."

Nell didn't have a lot of experience with antique dealers, but she knew the ones on television sometimes used the words *a rare find* when they were excited about something.

"What kind of rare find?" Byron Eslick asked suspiciously.

"Oh, very rare indeed!" Nell said. *Indeed.* That was another good word. She couldn't believe how convincing she sounded. Bucky and the Netherbeast watched her with approval.

Byron Eslick hesitated. Then he said, "I don't care. Goodbye."

"Wait!" Nell panicked. "We just want you to come by and take a look. That's all."

"No," the voice on the phone said. "You scam artists won't get a red cent out of me."

"We're not looking for money!" Nell said. "Just come by the house! I promise you'll see something remarkable!"

"What's remarkable," Byron Eslick said, "is that this conversation lasted as long as it did. Goodbye."

The line went dead. Nell looked up. Bucky and the Netherbeast wore the same disappointed expressions.

"Well . . . it was a good performance, anyway," Bucky said. "Who knows? Maybe Old Man Eslick will keep behaving himself. At least until the Florentines leave."

Suddenly, the stone wall the Netherbeast was sitting on split in half with a *crack!* The cat fled. At the same moment, all the flowers, including the ones in Nell's hand, withered and died.

Nell stared up at Rose Cottage. It had never looked angrier.

CHAPTER TWENTY-ONE
LULU STEPS IN

Lulu had bags under her eyes. The eyes that had been staring at Nell all morning as she did what she could to help make Rose Cottage presentable for the impending Florentines.

Nell tried to ignore her sister, even though everywhere she went, Lulu followed. Oh, she was *pretending* she wasn't following Nell around. But how many people did it take to change out the plain blue hand towels for special Sisterhood-approved embroidered towels? Or put out little soaps?

One. It took one person to do those things.

If there were a second person available, a person with a driver's license and a car, for example, *that* person might have been more help going into town to do the grocery shopping instead of making Aunt Jerry do it. But Nell just kept hanging towels and distributing soap as though there was nothing weird going on.

Finally, Lulu said, "What was that phone call you made yesterday?"

Nell hadn't been expecting that. "What . . . phone call?"

"What phone call?" Lulu shot back in a mocking voice.

"Get lost," Nell said, shaking out an embroidered towel and dropping it over the towel bar in a small upstairs bathroom.

"I'm sorry," Lulu said. Nell grunted, because it sounded like a real apology. Which was odd.

Lulu shrugged. "You don't have to tell me. I just . . . I know—*this*"—she gestured vaguely at everything—"hasn't been easy for you. Leaving the animal shelter and everything. And now your Junior Volunteers reference is riding on the Flying Florentines and Rose Cottage and *Ms. Tipton,* of all people. I mean, I know that's tough."

Nell froze. Was her sister actually being nice to her? She couldn't figure out how to get her motors to respond.

Lulu took a deep breath. "Are you okay, Nell? It's just that it sounded like you were trying to sell some antiques or something. But then you said you didn't want money. So . . ."

"Wow, you heard a lot," Nell said.

Lulu laughed. "Well, the window was open."

"Did Aunt Jerry hear?"

"I don't think so. Ms. Tipton definitely didn't; she was upstairs inspecting the baseboards."

Nell nodded. "Okay." Then she said, "I wasn't trying to, like, *steal* anything. I promise."

"Oh, I know you'd never steal," Lulu said. Sometimes Nell forgot that Lulu knew her pretty well. It felt kind of good.

She should tell her sister something about the phone call. Something true. But Nell couldn't tell the *whole* truth. Could she?

Nell decided to dip a toe into the lake of truth and see how it went. "Do you know who Old Mr. Eslick was? The man who used to live here?"

Lulu sat on the toilet lid, which was covered in frightening pink shag rug. "You mean the guy in the portrait downstairs? The one who looks like he spends his days yelling at people to get off his lawn?"

"Yeah." Nell leaned against rose-covered wallpaper. "The guy we called yesterday—that was his son. Mr. Eslick had a son who never spoke to him: Byron. Bucky and I thought . . ." *Okay, here's the big part. Here's where nice, old Lulu turns back into awful, new Lulu.* Nell cleared her throat. "We thought maybe the reason so many things are going wrong with the house is because of the—bad energy. The fact that Old Mr. Eslick was unhappy about being estranged from his son. Like, maybe the . . . spirit of Old Mr. Eslick is still here. You know, being upset."

There. It was out. Most of it.

Lulu was quiet. Then she said, "That makes sense, I guess."

Nell blinked. Was her sister really agreeing with her?

"I mean, if there's such a thing as a haunted house." Lulu shrugged. "Which I'm not saying there is." She looked around the bathroom. "But I think Aunt Jerry is in denial."

"You do?"

There was a moment of silence as Lulu seemed to study the wallpaper. Then she said, "Can I tell *you* something?"

Nell nodded. "Sure."

Lulu bit her lip. "So, I was down in the rumpus room yesterday."

"You *were?*" Nell's eyes widened.

"Yeah." Lulu hugged herself as though the bathroom had suddenly become cold. "There are some *seriously* bad vibes down there."

"I know," Nell said. She wondered if they were both remembering how Lulu had trapped her on the dark basement stairway the day they arrived.

"Anyway," Lulu said, "I was going to put a few books in the guest rooms. It's always nice when there are books around to read, right? And I went through the Sisterhood manual, and books aren't technically against the rules. So I went down to grab some and, well, okay, so first of all, your weird *cat* was down there. Lurking."

"He's good at lurking," Nell said.

Lulu gave her a dubious look. "He was all fluffed up and zooming around like his tail was on fire. Then he saw me—he made eye contact—and then he slowly swiveled his head until he was looking at that old couch. Like he wanted me to look at the couch, too."

Nell's mouth opened but she didn't say anything.

"So I did," Lulu went on. "And for just a second—a half-second—I . . . I *saw* someone. Sitting there." The color drained from her cheeks. "I swear, Nell. For a half-second, there was a geriatric dude on the couch, looking annoyed. Then *pfft!* Nothing."

Nell's heart jumped. "I think you saw the ghost of Old Man Eslick. I can see him, too." *I'm pretty sure the Netherbeast helps,* she thought, but she didn't say it. She didn't want to push Lulu too far, and she was already riding the line.

Lulu looked at the floor. "Look, I know you've been trying to talk about the stuff that's been happening for a while. I'm sorry I thought you were just being weird."

"Thanks."

"Well, for what it's worth, I believe you," Lulu said. "If you believe me."

Nell nodded. It felt comfortingly normal to believe each other.

Her sister leaned back. "The Flying Florentines are definitely not going to give a five-star review to a haunted inn."

"Nope."

"We've got to fix this, or all our plans go out the window, not to mention Aunt Jerry's business. And sanity." Lulu's eyes got kind of distant and she scrunched up her eyebrows. "You really think getting Brian Eslick here would, I don't know, make this ghost or whatever chill the heck out?"

"Byron. Yeah," Nell said. "But he said he wouldn't come."

"Huh." Lulu started chewing on one corner of her mouth, and her fingers tapped across her lap like she was playing an invisible piano. Nell recognized the signs right away: her sister was figuring something out. Usually—before this year, when she got *cool,* that is—it meant Lulu was working out how to wire up a radio or build a better gaming computer.

"Do you still have his number?" Lulu asked.

Nell blinked. "Byron Eslick's number? Yeah." She pulled the business card out of her pocket and handed it to her sister.

Lulu slid out her phone and tapped in the number.

"What are you doing?" Nell asked, but Lulu shushed her and flashed a crooked smile.

"Is this Mr. Eslick?" Lulu's voice was sharp and self-assured. The way Nell imagined a typewriter would sound if it could talk. "This is Tallulah Stoker, the manager of the Rose Cottage Inn."

Nell raised an eyebrow.

Lulu winked. Then she went on, "I wanted to personally apologize for the phone call you received yesterday. It was an unfortunate misunderstanding. You should never have been contacted."

"What?" Nell mouthed silently.

"That's right, a mistake," Lulu said. "You see, the rare find in question is definitely not available. In fact, we will not even be displaying it for the general public." There was a pause. Lulu's voice became even chillier. "No, I'm afraid that is not possible . . . Yes, Mr. Eslick, I realize you are Gordon Eslick's next-of-kin, but the fact remains that the house and all its contents were sold. Everything is now the property of the Cozy Corners Sisterhood of Inns, LLC . . . No, my assistant should not have called you yesterday, and we offer our sincere apologies for the error. We are not interested in selling anything from the estate. I wish you all the best. Please do not contact us again." She clicked off the call. Then she looked at Nell with a wide grin. "There. If that doesn't get Byron Eslick banging on our door, nothing will."

CHAPTER TWENTY-TWO
FAMILY REUNION

There was a sharp knock at the door just after lunch. Ms. Tipton had gone into town and Aunt Jerry was arranging the mugs at the self-serve coffee station in the kitchen according to the Sisterhood manual's specifications.

"I'll get it!" Nell and Lulu yelled at the same time. They raced down the front hall.

"Oof!" Nell tripped over something big lying on the floor. It was a knot of human and fur—Bucky and the Netherbeast, covered in dirt. "Bucky?" Nell said. "What are you doing here?"

Lulu looked back, her hand on the front doorknob. "What are you dipsticks doing? Get up!"

Bucky brushed himself off. He seemed a bit dazed. "I was outside working on the flowerbeds, but the Netherbeast seemed to think I should be here. In the house." He looked into the parlor where one of the bay windows was open. A trail of dirt led through the room and into the hall where they stood. "He was insistent."

Nell put her hands on her hips. "Did you *drag* Bucky in here?" She raised her eyebrows at the Netherbeast.

"Mow?" The Netherbeast raised his eyebrows back at Nell, until they were floating in the air six inches above his head.

Knock-knock-knock! The rapping was louder now. Lulu shot them a glare. "Are you two ready or what?"

Nell and Bucky straightened up and nodded. The Netherbeast quickly exploded all the dirt out of his fur, splattering the wainscoting. Lulu gave him a suspicious look but didn't say anything.

Then she took a deep breath and opened the door.

There, against the sunlight, was the man Nell had chased outside the café: Byron Eslick. His suit was rumpled and his tie was crooked, as though he had been in a rush. He scowled in a way that made him look just like his grumpy father.

"Can we help you?" Lulu said. She was blocking the doorway, but Byron pushed past her into the hall.

"All right, where is it?" he barked. "You!" He pointed at Nell. "I have rights, you know!"

Nell couldn't believe it. Lulu's plan had worked *perfectly*. Byron wouldn't listen when they'd *invited* him to Rose Cottage, but as soon as he was told he wasn't *allowed* to come—here he was, out of breath and red in the face as though he'd marched the whole way.

"It's in the rumpus room," Nell said.

Byron grinned craftily. "A-*ha!*"

Unfortunately, at that moment, Aunt Jerry came flitting in. "Oh!" she said, putting a hand to her sequined collar. "My goodness! I didn't know we had a visitor!"

Byron whirled around. "Are you the owner?"

"I—what?" Aunt Jerry looked like she was about to fall over. "Would you like to check in?"

"No, I would not like to check in!" Byron snapped. He jabbed a finger at Aunt Jerry. "You can try to fool me all you like, but I'll have you know, I *will* find out what you're hiding in the rumpus room! And then I'll have my lawyer down here so fast it'll make your head spin." His voice was as loud as a hurricane. The Netherbeast's ears flattened against his head as though they'd been blown back by the force. All his hair fell out with a *thbt.*

Aunt Jerry gaped at Byron Eslick. "The rumpus room?" She looked from Byron to Lulu with terrified eyes. "But . . . there's nothing in the rumpus room! Just junk."

"Lies!" Byron shouldered his way past everyone and thundered down the hall. "You can't keep it from me!"

"What on earth is going on?" Aunt Jerry whispered, her eyes bugging out of her head. "Oh, dear! I think I'm going to faint!"

"We'll handle it," said Nell. "Lulu, you'd better get Aunt Jerry a glass of water."

Lulu looked annoyed about her little sister bossing her around, but she nodded.

"And you," Nell said to the Netherbeast, "put your fur back on!"

Nell and Bucky hurried after Byron, who was already tramping down the stairs into the basement.

They found him standing completely still in the middle of the rumpus room, gaping at the rust-colored sofa. The Netherbeast zoomed across the room and perched on the back of the sofa, where the glowing form of an old man sat frowning.

"Holy cake pops," Bucky whispered. *"I can see him.* It's the ghost! It's Old Man Eslick! Oh, dear. Nell, do you see him?"

"Yeah," Nell whispered back. The Netherbeast was serene. His fur rippled blue and purple underneath the black. "I think the Netherbeast is helping all of us see him." She looked at Byron. "Including him."

All the blood had drained from Byron's face. He stared bug-eyed at the specter on the sofa.

Nell crept forward. "Mr. Eslick?"

But Byron took no notice of her. He seemed completely stunned. He kept opening and closing his mouth. Then he took a tentative step toward the sofa. "It can't be," he whispered.

Tingles ran up and down Nell's arms. She was witnessing something special. An impossible reunion between father and son. Two angry souls given another chance to find peace with each other. It was beautiful. She smiled at Bucky and crossed her fingers.

The ghost of Old Man Eslick scowled. He crossed his arms. "Byron."

Byron Eslick crossed his arms, too. "Father."

They glared at each other.

Uh-oh, Nell thought. "Byron, aren't you happy to see your dad?" she ventured.

This got Byron's attention. He wheeled around. "You! What do you know about this?"

Nell tripped back into the foosball table. "That's your father," she said, pointing.

"I know who it is!" Byron said.

"Byron," the ghost said in a mocking tone. Nell gave him a stern look. He stuck out his glowing tongue and made a fart noise. The Netherbeast made a fart noise, too.

"Hey!" Nell snapped. "Look, Byron—Ghost— this is supposed to be a touching family reunion."

"Is *that* what this is about?" Byron said. He pointed at the specter on the sofa. "You think I want a touching family reunion with *him?*"

"He's been tearing this house apart!" Nell said. "He's a menace!"

"Of course he is!" Byron said. "He's always been a menace! Why would I want to put up with it anymore now that he's dead?"

Nell turned to the ghost. "Well, aren't you happy to see your long-lost son?"

The ghost of Old Mr. Eslick jerked his head back. *"Byron?"* he said in a way that clearly meant, *"Him? Are you serious?"*

"Oh, dear." Bucky slumped down onto a stool next to the television. A shiver of beanbag beans cascaded onto his head from the shelf above.

Nell was furious. She stormed over to the glowing specter. "Are you kidding me right now?

You're down here throwing tantrums, exploding the light fixtures, terrorizing everyone, and it's *Byron, Byron, Byron* all day long, so we go to all the trouble of bringing your son here, and you're still not happy? What do you *want?*"

The ghost narrowed his eyes at her. He took a deep breath. Then he roared, "*Byron!*"

"Well, I've had quite enough of this," Byron said, straightening his tie. "I see you're just as dreadful as ever, Father," he said to the ghost. "I hope you're enjoying eternity in the rumpus room. It's almost as tacky as you are." Then he gave Nell and Bucky a dirty look. "Thank you, *charlatans,* for this *colossal* waste of time. I hope I never see any of you again."

The ghost of Old Mr. Eslick thumbed his nose at his son. Byron made a rude gesture back and tromped up the stairs, slamming the door behind him.

"So much for the touching family reunion." Bucky sighed.

"I don't understand," Nell said.

The ghost shrugged and rolled his eyes. "Byron."

Lulu came running down the stairs into the basement. "What happened? Byron Eslick just— holy *muffins* it's the ghost!" She gasped.

Everyone looked at her, including Old Mr. Eslick.

"Yeah, it's the ghost," Nell said, slouching onto the couch next to the translucent old man.

Lulu blinked a few times, but regained her composure. "Well, his son just peeled out of the driveway like the house was on fire. Nearly dinged my car." She put her hands on her hips. "What did you do to him?"

"Ask him!" Nell jutted a thumb at Old Mr. Eslick.

"Byron," he said darkly. "Byron, Byron, BYRON!"

And with the last *Byron,* the rumpus room exploded. Everything on a shelf came shooting off—board games and books and knickknacks went zooming across the room. The television keeled over onto its back. The plastic foosball players spun themselves into a frenzy, whirling right off their rods and bouncing off the walls. And every light bulb burst in a shower of hot glass.

"Run!" Bucky screeched. Everyone booked it for the stairs.

Back in the hall, they all stared down into the basement. All was quiet. "We were just trying to help you!" Nell shouted down.

From the darkness below, they heard the sound of someone blowing a ghostly raspberry.

The Netherbeast blew one back.

CHAPTER TWENTY-THREE
THE HOUSE FALLS APART

Overnight, all the glass panes fell out of the downstairs bay windows onto the lawn, cracking into a dozen pieces each. Every panel of wallpaper in the upstairs bedrooms peeled away, drifting onto the floor like huge discarded feathers. The furnace spluttered off. The back stairs fell apart. The walls bowed in, popping paintings onto the floor left and right. All the sinks filled with purple, grimy water, which spilled out over the tiles and crept under the doors into carpeted hallways. The new guest book somehow spontaneously combusted. Even Aunt Jerry's beloved old guest book with the puppies on the cover managed to fall out of its cupboard into a toilet.

At least the PA system exploded just before breakfast, halting the artificial birdsong and terrible soundtrack.

When Nell and Lulu came down in the morning, it was clear that everyone's hard work over the last few weeks had been for nothing. Tricking Byron Eslick into reuniting with his father had been a total disaster; the ghost of Old Mr. Eslick was as angry as ever. They were out of ideas, out of energy, and out of time: the Florentines would be flying in tomorrow morning.

"I don't understand," Aunt Jerry said despairingly, clutching her coffee mug with both hands. She, Lulu, and Nell sat at the table. Underneath, the Netherbeast batted at the cold puddles that had formed in the linoleum when the sink overflowed. Every few moments, a single plate would fall out of the cupboard for no reason and clatter onto the floor.

"Mr. Denver will be here soon," Lulu said. "We'll just have to fix and clean up what we can, before . . ."

"Yes," Aunt Jerry said in a voice like dry oats. "It's nice of him to come in on a Sunday, anyway."

Nell studied the curves in the wood grain of the table. On Sundays at home, the whole family would play Cardinal Mexican Train dominoes all afternoon. Right now, Nell felt like her future was a line of dominoes waiting to topple, *click,* one after the other. The Florentines would run screaming from the haunted B&B (click!); the Sisterhood of Whatever, LLC, would shut Rose Cottage down (click!); Lulu would have no job and Aunt Jerry would shatter like chandelier dropped from an airplane (CLICK!); Ms. Tipton would sabotage Nell's paperwork (CLICK CLICK!); and, with the biggest *CLICK!* of all, Shana would be proved right—Nell *wasn't* grown-up enough to really help at the shelter. Shana wouldn't need her anymore. Come fall, Nell would be stuck in Cape Green with no animals, no friends, and no sister.

"Ow!" Nell yelped as the Netherbeast sank a claw into her foot, all the way through her sneaker. A tear ran down her cheek, and it wasn't from the pain. Okay, it was partly from the pain. But partly it was because she suddenly realized that the worst thing of all was that when she went home, she'd have to give up the Netherbeast. After all, if she couldn't even be trusted to help at the shelter, how in the world would she convince Mom and Barb that she was responsible enough to have her own pet?

We're a team, she thought. *How can anybody break up a team?*

Just when it seemed like things couldn't get much worse, the front door swooshed open and there was the sound of someone clomping down the hall. Everyone looked up as Ms. Tipton burst into the kitchen. She stood with her hands on her hips. *"What,"* she said, frowning, "is all *this?* What has *happened* to this house?"

"I don't know! It just—" Aunt Jerry started, but Ms. Tipton cut her off.

"The Florentines will be here tomorrow! Rose Cottage is a *disaster!* This is *unacceptable.*" Ms. Tipton made a sharp noise like a chicken clucking. "I'm still waiting for the building inspector's report, but I can't *imagine* a *planet* on which this house would be up to code. I guess we'll just have to go with Plan B."

Aunt Jerry's eyebrows went up in surprise. "Plan B? What's Plan B? You never mentioned Plan B."

Ms. Tipton crossed her arms. "I'd hoped it wouldn't come to it," she said. But something in her voice made Nell suspicious that whatever Plan B was, it had been Ms. Tipton's Plan A all along. "You know that we at the Cozy Corners Sisterhood of Inns, LLC, place the utmost importance on making sure all our guests feel special and cozy." She pulled a pamphlet from her pocket and set it down on the table. "That's why we've been working hard to create the coziest, specialest inn in the whole world."

Nell looked at the glossy brochure. Across the top, in swirly letters made of cartoon flowers, it said:

PEACHY SKIES COTTAGE

THE COZIEST, SPECIALEST INN IN THE WHOLE WORLD!™
PART OF THE COZY CORNERS SISTERHOOD OF INNS, LLC

Below was a picture of a house covered in vines, with a thatched roof and diamond-paned windows, surrounded by flowers and windchimes and wicker furniture. There was something sickly sweet about it, Nell thought—like a cute woodland cottage out of a fairy tale that would actually turn out to be a child-eating house-monster in disguise before the end of the story.

"'Specialest' isn't a word," Lulu said, examining the brochure.

"It's marketing," Ms. Tipton snapped. "Anyway, Peachy Skies Cottage is the newest member of the Cozy Corners Sisterhood of Inns, LLC. It has professionally decorated rooms with frilly fabrics and tiny soaps, reclaimed wood furniture, and garden walks with birdsong and calming music piped over hidden loudspeakers day and night. In short, all the quaintness of a country inn without the *age* and *problems*."

"We have tiny soaps here," Nell said.

Ms. Tipton held up a finger. "Not as tiny as these. You can't get soaps this tiny around here. We have to import them."

"Those vines look plastic," Lulu said.

"They *are* plastic," Ms. Tipton said proudly. "No bugs! You see, Peachy Skies Cottage is truly perfect. And it's only one town away, in Deer Hill."

"Why are you telling us this?" Aunt Jerry asked.

"It's Plan B," Lulu said. "If Rose Cottage isn't up to snuff, Ms. Tipton's going to whisk the Florentines off to Peachy Skies instead."

"But how do we get our five-star review then?" Aunt Jerry asked.

"We don't," Nell said.

"I'd hoped it wouldn't come to that," Ms. Tipton said smugly.

Yes, you did, Nell thought. *You never wanted the Florentines to come to Rose Cottage. You just wanted an excuse to swoop in and whoosh them away and scoop up a five-star review for your new plastic palace. You were never going to give Aunt Jerry a good report. It's just icing on the cake that we've also got an angry ghost wrecking the decor.* But she didn't say any of it. What did it matter? If Ms. Tipton had been planning to close Rose Cottage down the whole time, what could any of them do about it?

The Netherbeast was giving Nell a disapproving stare. He couldn't read her mind, could he? That was *all* she needed.

"I'm sorry, everyone," Ms. Tipton said, in a voice that didn't sound sorry at all. "I'm just going to have to tell the Florentines that their reservation has been changed to Peachy Skies."

"But what about Rose Cottage?" Aunt Jerry asked, eyes wide.

"Rose Cottage had some good years," Ms. Tipton said. "But it's just not cutting it anymore. You're finished, Jerry. That's the hard truth."

And she walked out.

The sink made a loud *GLORP!* noise.

Nell, Lulu, and Aunt Jerry sat in silence. It felt like there was so much hard truth filling the sunny little kitchen that it was squashing all of them into their chairs.

A knock at the front door made everyone jump. But a second later, Mr. Denver's voice called out, "Hello?"

"We're in the kitchen," Lulu said in a monotone, staring into space. Aunt Jerry watched her coffee mug blankly. Nell studied a speck of blood popping through the top of her sneaker where the Netherbeast had punctured it.

Mr. Denver and Bucky stepped through the kitchen doorway looking bewildered. "What happened here?" Mr. Denver asked. "It looks like there was an earthquake or something."

Nell, Lulu, and Aunt Jerry looked up at them. Then the three of them shrugged at the same time.

Mr. Denver cleared his throat. "Hey, now. All right. I can see we've got some work to do before—" He looked at his watch. "—Oh, dear. Well, if we work fast, we can—" A teapot fell from the shelf above the door and bonked off his head. "Ow!"

"The Florentines aren't coming," Nell said.

"Oh." Mr. Denver blinked at her. "Any of that coffee left?"

Nell, Lulu, and Aunt Jerry silently pointed at the French press on the counter. Mr. Denver poured himself a cup, then sat glumly at the table.

After a moment, he said, "Don't suppose you have any sugar."

"Sugar is against Sisterhood rules," Aunt Jerry said in a faraway voice. "Only artificial sweetener is allowed."

"Here, Dad." Bucky pulled a couple sugar packets from his pocket.

His father smiled at him. "Always prepared, Starbuck. That's my boy."

As Bucky tossed the packets across the table, something else fell out of his pocket onto the linoleum.

"What's that?" Lulu asked.

Nell looked over as Bucky retrieved the object. "Oh. That's that old photo we found in the beanbag chair. The one of Mr. Eslick's son."

Bucky handed the photo to Lulu. "Not that it did us any good," he muttered.

"Oh, I remember," Lulu said.

Aunt Jerry cast a melancholy glance at the photo in Lulu's hands. The little boy with the neatly combed hair, clutching a teddy bear, stared out from the glossy surface. Aunt Jerry blinked. "Who did you say this was?"

Nell cleared her throat. "Byron Eslick. He's known as 'Scoot' Eslick now. Mr. Eslick's son. The—the unpleasant guy who was here yesterday."

Aunt Jerry took the photo and examined it, frowning. "No, that can't be right." She shook her head. "Wrong era."

The Netherbeast leaped onto the table and sniffed the photo suspiciously. Nell elbowed him aside. "What do you mean?"

"That man yesterday looked about my age. Our age." Aunt Jerry handed the photo to Mr. Denver. "Which makes sense; Mr. Eslick's son would be our generation. This picture looks much older, though."

"Definitely," Mr. Denver said. He raised one eyebrow at Bucky. "I may look like a fossil, son, but my baby pictures are in color."

"Well, we still take black and white pictures today," Lulu said. Nell remembered her sister had gone through a photography phase in middle school and had turned the downstairs bathroom into a darkroom. It had been very interesting and very annoying at the same time. A lot like Lulu herself.

"Tallulah, darling," Aunt Jerry said, sounding more like her old self, "*trust us* when we say this is not a photo from our era. It reminds me of the albums your mother and I used to look through from when our parents—your grandparents—were little."

"But that's not possible," Nell said. "Look at the back. It says, 'Byron.'"

"Hm." Aunt Jerry peered at the writing. "So it does." She handed the photo back to Bucky. "Well, I don't know what to tell you. That can't be Gordon Eslick's son."

"But it was taken here at Rose Cottage," Bucky said. "Look at the garden."

"Then it's more likely Gordon Eslick himself," Mr. Denver said. "He grew up here, you know."

"What?" Nell studied the face of the little boy. She'd seen the resemblance in the antique dealer when she first saw him in the café. But of course Scoot Eslick would look like his dad. She thought about the ghost in the rumpus room, and tried to picture the boy not just grown up, but old. And—she could see it. This little boy *could* be the grumpy specter wrecking Rose Cottage.

She could tell Bucky was thinking the same thing. He sighed and shook his head. "Then we're back where we started," he said. "What the heck does 'Byron' mean?"

"Who cares?" Aunt Jerry said exasperatedly. "What are we going to do about Rose Cottage?" A loud *GLOOP!* came from the sink and a geyser of slimy water spurted straight up out of the drain. It rained down onto the Netherbeast, who yowled, then wrung his own midsection out like a wet towel. Nell shot him a look. Luckily, the others hadn't noticed.

Mr. Denver wrapped his fingers around his coffee mug. "I'm not sure there's much we *can* do."

Aunt Jerry flopped over onto the table. Her glittery glasses slid from where they'd been perched in her purple hair. "I'm ruined! Without the Florentines, the Cozy Corners Sisterhood of Inns, LLC, will close Rose Cottage forever! What will become of me?"

Mr. Denver sipped his coffee in a dazed way. Amazingly, Lulu had nothing to say. Things seemed hopeless.

But Nell thought and thought. She went around one way, then the other. She looked at everyone slumped at the table like a gathering of deflated balloons. And then she saw the Netherbeast looking at *her,* his cosmic yellow eyes flashing as if to say, *Well?*

Well? It's up to you now, Nell. What are you going to DO about it?

Nell Stoker brushed a thumb over the old photograph. She cleared her throat. Everyone looked up.

"What's up?" Bucky asked.

"I was just thinking . . ." Nell began. "I mean—if the Florentines *did* come here—if we could convince them—and if they *did* leave a five-star review, well . . . how could the Sisterhood close us down? They couldn't. If we could just fix Rose Cottage before tomorrow." Everyone looked skeptical. But Nell leaned forward, and the truth tumbled out. "Aunt Jerry, Mr. Denver—you should know: there's an angry ghost in the basement. Old Mr. Eslick. That's why all this is happening."

"Nell, shut up!" Lulu hissed. "Remember how *fragile* some of us are! And we've already had the worst morning ever!" She shot a glance at Aunt Jerry, who looked stricken.

Nell threw back her shoulders. "I believe we're stronger than you think," she said. "All of us."

Aunt Jerry gave a little cry and the blood drained from her face. "A . . . did you say a—? Was that what you were trying to tell me before? Oh, Nell! *Oh!*"

"Eleanor, please don't upset your aunt," Mr. Denver said in a severe voice. "Jerry, there's no such thing as—ow!" Another teapot bonked off his head.

"I didn't know we even *had* two teapots," Lulu said, looking around.

"It's true, Dad," Bucky said. "There's a ghost, and I've seen him." His father started to interrupt, but Bucky went on. "Think about it—the windows, the shingles, the porch—"

"The piano," Aunt Jerry whispered.

"Right, the piano," Bucky said. "You don't

want to admit it, but you *know* something weird is going on here."

At that moment, all the curtains slipped off their hangers and fell to the floor with a *floop*.

"But what that *means*," Nell said, un-mooselike, "is that our problems have a cause—and a solution. We have to soothe Mr. Eslick's ghost. Then he'll leave the house alone, and Rose Cottage can go back to being the kind of cute little bed and breakfast that travel influencers love. That's what Bucky and I have been trying to do. We just haven't figured out how." She left out the part about her cat secretly being a Netherbeast. There wasn't enough space in the whole house for that big a truth.

Mr. Denver stared at her. Nell could tell he wanted to be stern—he was good-natured and she figured he didn't have much patience for people who made others upset. But he didn't seem to know what to say.

Lulu looked as though she'd seen a ghost. Well, *another* ghost. She looked as though Nell had walked up and smacked her in the face with a dead fish. Her gaze kept flitting from Nell to Aunt

Jerry, as though she expected their fragile aunt to splinter into shards before their very eyes.

Aunt Jerry was googly-eyed and exhaling in this *tight* kind of way, with a long squeaking noise. When all her air had squeaked out, there was a pause. Nell wondered if her aunt would just keel over then and there.

But instead, Aunt Jerry asked, "So what can we do? H—how can we appease Mr. *You Know* . . . This gh—gh—" She grimaced and pointed downward in the direction of the basement.

"We don't have much time," said a small voice. Nell was surprised that it belonged to Mr. Denver. He blinked, as though even he were surprised that he was talking.

"Time?" Aunt Jerry said. "What do you mean?"

"The Florentines are still flying in tomorrow," Nell said. "They're still planning to stay here, unless Ms. Tipton talks them out of it. We have to make sure they come, no matter what she says. Aunt Jerry, can you call them? Reassure them that we're ready for them?"

"Oh! Yes. Right away."

"We can still fix this," Nell went on. "If we *do* get a five-star review, there's no way the Sisterhood will close us down. The Florentines' fans would throw a fit."

"The Sisterhood does pay close attention to Internet trends," Aunt Jerry murmured.

Now Lulu spoke up, with the old swagger back in her tone. "Okay. Step one. The ghost clearly wants something. We have to figure out what."

"It's something to do with this photograph," Bucky said. "The Neth—uh, *Nell* seems pretty sure about that."

Everyone looked at Nell.

"Well," she said, "I do have one thought. I mean . . . The only person in town we haven't asked about this photo is—the one person who's, apparently, actually in it."

✦ ✦ ✦

CHAPTER TWENTY-FOUR
BYRON

"**Y**ou want to go down *there?* With *him?*" Bucky said.

Everyone stood at the top of the basement stairs. The air was so cold it made them shiver. There was a strange kind of swirliness to the shadows below them now, as though they were thick water flowing and glooping around invisible rocks. The Netherbeast was sniffing suspiciously. Every once in a while, a spark would crackle through the air, causing the cat's grimy black fur to stand on end.

"It's awfully dark," said Aunt Jerry.

"I'm not sure those stairs are sound," said Mr. Denver. The righthand railing popped off its supports and creaked overboard.

Nell was firm. "There's no backing out now! The Florentines will be here tomorrow!"

"Maybe I shouldn't have called them," Aunt Jerry said.

"You did the right thing," Nell said. "Now we have to ask Mr. Eslick about the photo. It's our only chance to save Rose Cottage."

"But all he says is 'Byron!'" Bucky whined.

Lulu put her hands on her hips. "Nell is right. Let's go."

Her sister's support made Nell feel all warm and fuzzy—for about two seconds, until Lulu gave her a rude shove. Nell almost went tumbling down the stairs, but she caught her balance and hopped down, frigid air eddying around her. The rest of the group followed nervously.

"Help them see," Nell whispered to the Netherbeast. "Help them all see Mr. Eslick the way you helped before." The cat seemed to glitter for a moment in the darkness.

None of the light switches worked, so they felt their way into the rumpus room, which was illuminated by an otherworldly glow. A strong breeze blew from all sides. Books flew like awkward birds, drawers flapped, and an old change jar toppled from a shelf, flinging its coins around at great speeds.

"Oh!" Aunt Jerry said, clutching the collar of her shirt. "Why is it so breezy? Should it be this breezy?"

"Should it be this *haunted?*" said Mr. Denver, pointing a trembling finger.

There, in the center of the room, sat the ghost of Old Man Eslick. His mouth was twisted into a scowl that was somehow bigger than his face. His eyes glowed as bright as white lasers. The sofa gleamed like fire all around him.

"Ow!" Lulu said as a dime plinked off her forehead.

"Nell was right," Aunt Jerry murmured.

"Yeah," Bucky said.

Nell reached for the pull cord of a table lamp. Luckily, it turned on. This caused the ghost to pause and turn his incandescent head in her direction. His eyes rolled from one person to the next.

Mr. Eslick seemed taken aback by all these visitors. The air stopped whipping and all the levitated objects fell onto the carpet with a smattering of thuds. An open hardbound dictionary fell squarely on top of the Netherbeast, who hissed and burst into flames. Bucky quickly covered the whole mess with a blanket, which the Netherbeast immediately started shredding.

Nell took another step toward the couch. "Uh—hi, Mr. Eslick."

The specter narrowed his eyes at her.

"Can I sit with you?"

Mr. Eslick shook his head and crossed his arms.

Nell sat anyway. Mr. Eslick turned away crabbily.

"Maybe you shouldn't touch the ghost," Mr. Denver said. He stood behind the foosball table, gripping the handles.

"You *can't* touch him," Nell said. "There's nothing there." To demonstrate, she pushed a finger right through Mr. Eslick's glowing head.

This clearly annoyed the ghost. He scooted away from Nell on the couch, flaring his nostrils.

"Sorry," Nell said. "That wasn't polite of me"

Mr. Eslick glared.

Nell took a deep breath. "Look, we were wondering if you'd take a look at this picture." She held out the photograph.

For a moment, the apparition just stared at her, squinting and flaring his nostrils. Then he turned his head and looked down at the photo.

Instantly, the air in the room became warmer, like a summer day.

"Oh!" Aunt Jerry said softly. She relaxed the fingers at her collar.

Mr. Eslick stared at the photo of the little boy clutching his teddy in Rose Cottage's beautiful garden. He reached out a luminous hand as though to touch it.

"That's you, isn't it?" Nell asked.

"Byron," the ghost whispered.

Nell sighed. "It's not, Mr. Eslick. That's not your son. It's you. It's Gordon."

"Byron," the ghost said quietly, opening and closing his translucent fingers, trying to grasp the photograph. He turned to Nell. Now his spectral eyes were half as big as his entire head, full and shining. Starlight dripped down his gleaming cheeks.

"He's crying!" Bucky said.

"Of course he is," said Aunt Jerry. "He's very sad, poor man."

"But why?" asked Mr. Denver.

And suddenly, Nell understood. "Because," she said, blinking at the photo, "he's not the only one in this picture after all."

A little boy, hair combed, shoes polished, clutching a teddy bear.

Clutching a teddy bear.

Nell pointed, then looked into Mr. Eslick's large, bright eyes. *"That's* Byron, isn't it? Your bear?"

The ghost nodded. He spoke in a rusty voice tinged with sadness. "Byron."

CHAPTER TWENTY-FIVE

UP IN FLAMES

"All this over an eighty-year-old teddy bear?" Mr. Denver said. "What are we supposed to do—look for it? It could be anywhere!"

"The attic?" Nell asked.

"Maybe local antique shops," Lulu said.

"It's hopeless. Hopeless!" Aunt Jerry cried. But she hadn't shattered. She was still vertical, sitting primly on an embroidered armchair in the front parlor. Groans and smashes from the rumpus room reverberated all around the house. The Florentines were going to be flying into a nightmare if the ghost couldn't be pacified soon. And even then, the bed and breakfast would be looking pretty shabby. *Maybe we can win them over with our sparkling personalities*, Nell thought.

"I should never have invited you girls," Aunt Jerry said. "All of this started just when you got here!"

When you got here . . . Nell's heart jumped in her chest. The Netherbeast! Could he have been the cause of the terrible troubles at Rose Cottage? Nell could only imagine what the destructive cat would do to a delicate antique toy if he happened to find it . . .

The Netherbeast was sitting on the hearth, pawing through the fireplace ashes and making a sooty mess all over the floor. To top it off, the dust was making him sneeze big green booger globs all over the bricks and the walls.

Nell's stomach sank. What if it had been the Netherbeast who upset the ghost?

"But wait," Nell realized. "Aunt Jerry, you said the strange occurrences started happening before we got here. The staff had already quit by the time we arrived."

"Well . . ." Aunt Jerry made a dismissive gesture, like those kinds of details didn't matter. "It wasn't *long* before."

"But I don't understand it," Bucky said, throwing his hands up. "Mr. Eslick must have lost his teddy ages ago. Ms. Moufflon, you've managed Rose Cottage for years. Nothing has changed!"

"Right," Aunt Jerry's glitter glasses wobbled. "It's *certainly* never been—you know—" She lowered her voice. "*Haunted.*"

"Maybe it's that Ms. Tipton," Lulu said bitterly. She was sitting cross-legged on an overstuffed ottoman, braiding its tassels. "Maybe she brings out the bad energy in a place."

"You have been working too hard, Jerry," Mr. Denver added. "You're stressed out. Can any travel influencers really be that important?"

Something clicked in Nell's brain. "That's what's different," she said. "That's what changed. Aunt Jerry—you said Ms. Tipton had you doing some extra sprucing up. Cleaning up junk. Just before we got here."

Aunt Jerry pushed her glasses up the bridge of her nose. "So?"

"So," Nell said, "you didn't happen to get rid of—"

"Oh!" Aunt Jerry put a hand to her mouth. "Oh, *Nell!* Oh, *no!*"

Everyone stared at her. The Netherbeast flopped into a sitting position in a cloud of ash and goggled.

Aunt Jerry swallowed. She wove her trembling fingers together. Then she spoke in the tiniest voice in the world, like a mouse apologizing. "I . . ." she said. "I remember now. I *did* get rid of an old—I guess it was a stuffed animal." She paused. Nobody said a word. "There was this cardboard box in the basement. It had been shoved into a damp corner of the rumpus room." She cleared her throat. "I'd never throw out someone's beloved bear!" she exclaimed. "But you have to understand—all that stuff was *ruined*. It was a box of tatty old socks full of holes and a few books missing half their pages— and this old bear that had just *disintegrated*. Every bit of it was white and green and black with mold." Her gaze flitted nervously around the parlor. "There was nothing left to save! It would have made people sick! So I . . . I got rid of the whole bunch of it."

Nell leaned forward. "Where? Where did you put the box, Aunt Jerry?"

"The town dump!" Mr. Denver said.

"It might still be near the top of the pile!" Bucky said.

"Where is the dump?" Nell asked, gears turning. "We can go right now!"

201

But Aunt Jerry shook her head. "I didn't throw the box out," she said. Her wide-eyed gaze moved to the large fireplace where the Netherbeast had been digging and sneezing for the last fifteen minutes. Ash was spread thin all over the hearth bricks, and nothing remained but a handful of charred lumps no bigger than marbles. "I'm sorry to say," Aunt Jerry whispered. ". . . I burned it all up."

CHAPTER TWENTY-SIX
OUT OF TIME

Lulu looked at her watch. "The Florentines will be here in twenty-two hours."

"We'll just have to send them to Peachy Skies after all," Mr. Denver said.

Aunt Jerry's eyes were wild. "We can't! I'll be ruined! And Lulu's job!"

And Nell's Junior Volunteers, Nell thought.

Mr. Denver sighed and glanced at the grandfather clock. "Bucky and I should get home. Chumbles needs walkies."

"I walked him an hour ago," Bucky said.

"Well, we all need some sleep," Mr. Denver said. The hands of the grandfather clock popped off and zoomed through the air toward his face. He ducked sadly and the clock hands stuck into the wall behind him.

"But, Dad, it's not even noon—" Bucky said.

"I'm sorry, Starbuck." Mr. Denver put an arm around his son's shoulders. "We did our best." He looked around the old house, which was still falling apart faster than anyone could put it back together.

"Besides, do you really want the Florentines to set foot in here?" Lulu asked. "If they're not going to love it, they might as well not come." The ceiling fan dropped with a *thwack!* onto the rug between them, making everyone jump, including the Netherbeast, who rocketed to the ceiling and clung there with all four paws.

Aunt Jerry looked as though she were about to cry.

Nell cleared her throat. "We've got to try," she honked.

Aunt Jerry gave her a grateful look. "Nell's right. We've got to try."

They all looked at Mr. Denver. He shrugged. Then he smiled. "Okay. You're the boss. Where do we start?"

"I . . . I . . ." Aunt Jerry shivered.

Lulu stood up. "Okay. Start with the front yard and work backward in a path to the Florentines' room," she said crisply. "Forget the kitchen and parlor; shut the doors. Haul all the debris into the bushes, or fling it down the basement stairs. Get the pictures back up. Grab rugs from the unused rooms upstairs and get them over the water stains. Hang the curtains at the front back up—they'll hide the broken windows." She barked orders like a head chef, or a fire chief, or the president of an important company, Nell thought.

"Now that's an assistant manager!" Aunt Jerry said.

Lulu pointed at Bucky. "Fish the old guest book out of the toilet and dry it with the hair dryer, then put it on the front desk. Make sure the cute puppies are visible."

Bucky saluted. "On it!" He ran out of the room.

"I'll work on the Florentines' room," Lulu said. "Nell, sweep up all this ash. And—" She paused, glaring at the Netherbeast. "Do something about that thing on the ceiling."

Aunt Jerry and Mr. Denver snapped into action. In a flash, everyone had dispersed to their duties, leaving Nell and the Netherbeast in the parlor.

Nell was astonished. Lulu's bossiness was actually good for something. Who knew?

The floor vibrated as the ghost in the basement raged. *Maybe he'll tire himself out,* Nell thought. She sighed. *Not likely.*

She looked at the cat fixed to the ceiling. He was digging the plaster out in tiny chunks, creating a mini moon surface pocked with craters.

"Get down from there," Nell said. "We've got work to do."

The Netherbeast blew a raspberry.

"That is a *very* rude habit," Nell said. "Anyway, we need to clean this up."

The Netherbeast detached himself and plummeted to the floor. Then he trotted back over to the fireplace and started pawing through the ashes again.

"Hey, cut it out," Nell said. "I've got to sweep that!" She grabbed a little broom and shovel from their brass stand next to the hearth and got to work. But no matter how quickly she swept, the Netherbeast would get into the ashes again and fling them all over the floor.

"Ugh!" Nell grunted. "You are *impossible!*" She flopped down onto the hearth. "Can't you stop being weird for ten minutes?"

But he couldn't. The Netherbeast was proud of his weirdness, just as Nell used to be proud of hers. As annoying as he was, part of Nell wished she could be more like him.

And then it hit her. *Really* hit her. The dominoes were falling. She was going to lose the Netherbeast, just as Old Mr. Eslick had lost Byron the bear.

Nell hardly ever cried, but she felt tingles at the corners of her eyes just thinking about how sad the ghost in the basement must be. For the first time, she understood what it would feel like to lose your best friend. If only the Netherbeast could reverse time; if only they could go back and stop Aunt Jerry from burning up that old box of junk. But Nell knew in her bones that some things were impossible. Byron was gone.

She slumped against the legs of the fancy parlor couch. *All right,* she thought. *We can't travel through time. But what* can *we do to get rid of this ghost? What powers does the Netherbeast have?* She made a list in her mind.

    • **Stinkiness.** *Can ghosts smell? Doesn't seem likely.*

    • **Frightening appearance.** *Huh! Not even the Netherbeast can scare the scariest thing in the house.*

    • **Razor claws and needle teeth.** *Would be helpful in defending us if Mr. Eslick were an ax murderer, but not much use since he's already dead.*

    • **Doesn't care what people think.** *No help at all, since all of this is about what the Florentines think. Why does so much always depend on following other people's rules?*

    • **Shapeshifting.** *The Netherbeast could become the fanciest, glitteriest scarf there ever was! But that probably wouldn't make up for the tantrum-throwing ghost. Wait—maybe he could disguise himself as Byron the bear? . . . No. Ghostly Mr. Eslick would definitely know the difference between his special bear and a Netherbeast impostor.*

Nell sighed. If only *she* had special powers. But she was just a weird, tick-averse kid from

Cape Green who occasionally found lost pets . . .

Found.

Lost.

Pets.

Nell sat up. She *did* have a special power. Shana knew it. Lulu knew it. The Netherbeast probably knew it, too. Her power was *reuniting*.

She jumped to her feet. "I have an idea!"

The Netherbeast paused. He gave Nell an expectant stare.

"We're going to have to work together," she said. The Netherbeast swiveled his ears forward. Nell went on, "You know how you can kind of . . . *help* people to see ghosts?"

The cat blinked. Nell wasn't sure if that gesture meant anything or not. But the Netherbeast continued to wait patiently for what she was going to say next.

"Well," she said, "I think I can help *you* see Byron's ghost."

The Netherbeast tilted his head skeptically.

Nell swallowed. "Look, I know it sounds bananas. But I think you've been messing around with those ashes for a reason, even if you don't know it. I think Byron is still *in* there. Some part of him. And I'm very good at finding lost things."

The Netherbeast was so skeptical his head tilted all the way upside down and fell off.

Nell knelt down. "A month ago, I wouldn't have believed ghosts were real. Or that *Netherbeasts* were real. But I did know that feelings were real. And it's like—in some way, Mr. Eslick's ghost is a feeling. I know teddy bears aren't alive, but there are so many feelings inside them, you know? It makes them alive in a way." She pointed to the heaps of ashes strewn around the fireplace and hearth. "Byron the bear is in there somewhere. I'm sure of it. Can you look for him?"

The Netherbeast's head yawned. His body stretched lazily.

"Look, I'm telling you I need your help." Nell put her hands on her hips. "I'm not just *anybody*, you know."

The Netherbeast's head raised its eyebrows.

"That's right," Nell said confidently. "I know I can't make the sky turn black or dissolve my own bones or turn into a piece of fruit. I'm just a kid

with knobby elbows. But your life wasn't so hot when we met, either, was it? Alleys and garbage and *rain*."

The Netherbeast's body shrugged.

"You might fool everyone else, but you never fooled me," Nell went on. "I *saw* you. Just like I saw Mr. Eslick when nobody else could without your help. We're a couple of weirdos who go together. Face it." She stuck out her hand. "I'm your *partner*."

The Netherbeast looked at Nell's outstretched hand. He rolled his head back up onto his body and took a step closer. His whiskers quivered. Then he *CHOMPED!* her fingers.

"Ow!" Nell frowned as the punctures started bleeding. "I'm going to take that as an agreement."

The Netherbeast turned to the soot-blackened fireplace. He sniffed. He rolled. He sneezed goopy green boogers. Nell watched. She didn't say a word, but she *thought*. She focused on Byron. *Come out, Byron. I know you're in there.*

The cat nosed over every inch of the fireplace. Suddenly, when he came to an ashy place in the back corner, his tail stuck straight out, *zing!* His fur frizzed. And he took a deep breath—so deep that he inflated to twice his original size. Nell held her own breath.

Slowly, slowly, the Netherbeast exhaled. Tiny particles of ash swirled. And behind the ash, or through it, or under it—Nell wasn't sure— something began to glow. At first, it was as though someone far away were shining a flashlight into the sooty corner of the fireplace. Then it got brighter and brighter. It started to take shape—a round body, round head, and two round ears.

By the time the Netherbeast had exhaled all his breath, there sat the shining form of a child's teddy bear.

"Mo-wow," the Netherbeast said, which clearly meant, *Well, would you look at that?*

"Byron!" Nell said. The bear turned its head in her direction, which made her jump. "Ack! Oh! You can move." The bear continued to stare at her. "That's . . . kind of creepy."

"Ffffft!" the Netherbeast hissed. The bear swiveled its head completely around until it was staring at the Netherbeast. The cat's eyes widened. He seemed taken aback.

"Behave," Nell muttered to the Netherbeast. "We don't want to lose him."

The Netherbeast sat back on his haunches and proceeded to bathe his tail in a pouty sort of way.

Nell crept forward on her hands and knees, not caring about the ash and soot. "Hey, little guy," she cooed at the glowing spirit of the teddy bear. The bear stared at her silently. It was unnerving. Nell cleared her throat. "I know someone who misses you an awful lot. Will you come with me?"

The bear stared.

Nell reached out a hand. "Here, I'll help you." She gently slid her fingers beneath the shining stuffed animal. But when she lifted her hand, it went right through. "Oh," she said. "Right. You're a ghost."

The bear stared.

Nell didn't know what to say. She stared back.

The Netherbeast stopped bathing his tail and stared.

Nobody moved.

"Well," Nell said. "What do we do now?"

"Ah-*hem*," came a throat-clearing sound from the Netherbeast. He trotted over to the ghost of Byron the bear. Then he opened his mouth and lunged for one of the stubby little glowing arms.

CHOMP!

CHAPTER TWENTY-SEVEN
A BOY AND HIS BEAR

"**H**ey!" Nell snapped as the Netherbeast *chomped* down on Byron's translucent arm.

But the cat just raised his eyebrows and lifted his head—and the teddy bear with it.

"Oh!" Nell said. "You can touch ghosts!"

The Netherbeast shrugged modestly.

"You have so many cool powers," Nell said, getting to her feet. She wasn't sure, but it seemed like the tips of the Netherbeast's ears turned a little pink under his grubby fur. "Come on, we've got to bring Byron down to the rumpus room and give him back to Old Mr. Eslick."

They trotted out of the parlor and headed down the hall. Around them was nothing but chaos—Aunt Jerry flapping carpets out windows, Lulu standing dangerously on her tiptoes on a stool while hanging curtains, Mr. Denver furiously vacuuming, and Bucky sweeping up ceramic shards as fast as the plates could hurl themselves out of their kitchen cupboards.

"Hey, everybody?" Nell's voice was the tiny squeak of a baby moose. It was completely covered up by the hum of the vacuum, the tinkle of plates, and the flapping of carpets.

"Moww." There was a muffled sound from the end of the hall, as though a cat were trying to get Nell's attention with a ghost bear stuffed in his mouth.

"I'm coming." Nell straightened her shoulders. "Excuse me!" she honked. *"Hey, everyone! Listen up!"*

The vacuuming, tinkling, and flapping stopped. Everyone poked their heads into the hallway.

Nell cleared her throat. "We, uh . . ." she said. "We found Byron."

"Really?" Lulu said. She sounded impressed.

"How?" Aunt Jerry asked.

"I'll show you." Nell led them around the corner to the door to the basement, where the Netherbeast was waiting. A glowing teddy bear dangled from his jaws.

"I don't believe it!" Aunt Jerry put a hand to her collar. "It's a—*ghost bear!*"

"He was still in the fireplace," Nell said.

"That's one . . . *special* cat," Lulu said. She gave her sister a suspicious look, but didn't elaborate.

"Anyway," Nell said, "we can give him back to Old Man Eslick now."

"And maybe all this nonsense will finally stop and I can have my home back!" Aunt Jerry cried.

They found the ghost raging in the rumpus room. The shelves were empty. Everything had been flung onto the floor—board games, books, knickknacks, a mug full of pencils, someone's forgotten collection of shot glass souvenirs from sunny vacation spots. The air was so cold that icicles hung from the lampshades and underneath the foosball table. In the middle of the mess sat Mr. Eslick, waving his ghostly arms and kicking his skinny, glowing legs.

"Hello, Mr. Eslick," Nell said. A plastic soccer player winged off her shoulder. Aunt Jerry jumped as a record cabinet fell onto its side. Lulu swatted aside an old paperback copy of *Peril at End House* as it sailed toward her nose.

"We have something for you!" Nell gave the Netherbeast a nod. "Okay. Go for it."

The cat trotted toward the rust-colored sofa, the translucent bear swinging from his mouth.

But Mr. Eslick didn't pay any attention. *"Gwaaaah!"* he wailed, sending his ghostly dentures spinning through the air. Suddenly, with a massive *groan*, the walls of the rumpus room began to buckle. Plaster rained from the ceiling in chunks.

"It's coming down!" Aunt Jerry cried. "Get to the stairs!"

They ran for it. Then *FLUMP!* A huge oak bookshelf toppled over in front of the doorway. They were trapped.

"Help me move this!" Lulu gripped one end of the heavy bookshelf and tried to drag it. Nell and Aunt Jerry grabbed hold. The walls creaked and rumbled. Cracks shot up from the floor, splitting the wood paneling. A chunk of ceiling crashed down, knocking Nell over.

"Squashed by a rumpus room!" Aunt Jerry put her hands over her eyes. "I was always afraid this was how it would end!"

"Cover your heads!" Lulu yelled. The room shook. The walls groaned. The ceiling shuddered. Nell curled into a ball and took a deep breath. She closed her eyes tight.

Then, suddenly, everything went quiet.

Nell peeked from one eye.

The walls were still up. The ceiling had stopped disintegrating. She stared at the center of the room, where the ghost of Old Man Eslick had been camped out on the rust-colored sofa.

Only now he was gone. Nell blinked and got to her feet. "Look," she whispered. Lulu and Aunt Jerry raised their heads.

"Oh!" Aunt Jerry murmured.

"Holy crab cakes," Lulu said.

In the spot where Old Mr. Eslick had been now sat something else: the glowing specter of a little boy. He was holding a ghostly teddy bear.

Nell slowly crossed the room. "Mr. Eslick?" she said. The little boy didn't respond. "Gordon?"

The ghost of the boy looked up. He held up the bear. A wide grin spread across his face. "Byron!"

"Yeah," Nell said, smiling. "Byron."

The boy hugged the bear. Specks of light jumped from his fingertips and the tops of his ears and the ends of his toes. He looked at Nell. "Thank you."

Nell blinked, and both boy and bear were gone.

Instantly, the rumpus room felt warmer. And brighter. It wasn't brighter with light, but it *felt* brighter to Nell. It was like opening a heavy curtain and letting the sunlight stream into a dark room, but the sunlight was a feeling.

On the floor next to the sofa, the Netherbeast sat vigorously cleaning his butt.

"Good job," Nell whispered. The cat didn't look up, but he started purring like a jet engine.

✦ ✦ ✦

CHAPTER TWENTY-EIGHT
CONDEMNED

It took all of them working together to get the oak bookshelf upright again, and the rumpus room was a mess, but at least the basement, and the rest of the house, was still structurally sound. It wasn't the prettiest it had ever been, but the walls were standing. They had something to work with, and with no more ghostly destruction on the horizon, maybe now they really could get Rose Cottage back into shape. Maybe, just maybe, there was still time.

As soon as everyone got upstairs again, the phone rang. Lulu picked it up at the front desk. "Rose Cottage Bed and Breakfast. How may I help you? . . . Oh, hello." All of a sudden, Lulu's voice became shrill, like when Mom and Barb made her bring Nell along when she did fun things with her friends. "Wait, what? What did you tell them?"

"What's the matter?" Aunt Jerry asked. She scuttled over and took the phone from Lulu. "Hello? . . . Ms. Tipton, what do you want? . . . They're what? When? For how long? *What?* But— what about us? What about my nieces? You *what?* You can't . . . But . . . but . . . I see." Slowly, she hung up the receiver.

"You can't let her do this!" Lulu said.

Nell raced to the desk. "What happened?"

"That was Ms. Tipton," Aunt Jerry said. She cleared her throat. "The Florentines flew in early, apparently. And guess who was waiting for them at the airport?"

"What's going on?" Mr. Denver emerged from the kitchen with Bucky.

Aunt Jerry gave everyone a wide-eyed look. "Well, you see—"

"Ms. Tipton has kidnapped the Florentines!" Lulu said.

Everyone gasped.

"Call the police!" Mr. Denver said.

"Well, not exactly *kidnapped*," Lulu admitted. "But close enough! She took them to that awful new inn, Peachy Skies!"

Everyone looked at Aunt Jerry. "It's true," she said. "They're all unpacked and everything. Ms. Tipton says they're enjoying fruity beverages by the wading pool even as we speak." She ran her fingers over the cute puppy guest book. "The Florentines are not coming here after all. Not now, not ever."

Nell's jaw dropped. "But—but we *found Byron!*"

"Yes. You did a wonderful thing that made poor Mr. Eslick very happy," Aunt Jerry said with a sad smile. "And I know it made Rose Cottage happy, too."

"Look, Nell," Lulu said hopelessly. "We never would have gotten a five-star review. Ms. Tipton knew that all along."

Bucky looked at Nell. Nell looked at Bucky. But there was nothing they could do.

"It's getting late, Jerry," Mr. Denver said. "Hey . . . try to get a good night's sleep, okay?" And he steered his son out the door.

The newly painted front door closed behind them with a soft click. Aunt Jerry collapsed into an armchair behind the desk. Lulu's shoulders slumped.

Nell shuffled over to them. "Did Ms. Tipton say anything about Rose Cottage?"

The look on Aunt Jerry's face told her everything she needed to know. And it wasn't good.

"How *could* she?" Lulu said, smacking the desk, which made Aunt Jerry jump. "We've worked so hard! I *need* this job! Mom and Barb can barely pay the tuition loans! How will I afford my books? The dorm?"

Nell swallowed. "What about my . . ." *Junior Volunteers. Proving I'm responsible. Keeping the Netherbeast.* Lulu leaned in, all ears. But for some reason, Nell couldn't finish her sentence.

"Oh, girls," Aunt Jerry said forlornly. "Nell . . . Ms. Tipton already sent your paperwork in. She . . . did not give you a good reference. I'm afraid it's just bad news for all of us."

Click. Nell felt the last domino fall. Her bad report was on its way to Shana right now. That was that.

Then a strange thing happened. All of a sudden, Nell didn't mind so much about the Junior Volunteers. She realized grown-ups could be just as fragile or awkward or mean or *weird* as kids. Maybe she *wasn't* ready. Maybe she wasn't good with people yet. But she would be someday. Nell knew that now, and she was going to keep trying.

What she *was* good at was being a team with the Netherbeast. Losing her first, best cat, even if he wasn't really hers and even if he wasn't really a cat—that's what wasn't fair. Aunt Jerry losing Rose Cottage—that wasn't fair. And as Nell looked at Lulu, she realized the only thing more infuriating than seeing her older sister flap away to college without her was seeing her with her wings tied.

"Mr. Denver's right. It's late," Aunt Jerry said. "Let's try to get some sleep."

The next morning, Aunt Jerry drifted onto the porch, staring at her phone as Nell swept away pine needles in the sunshine. "It's over," she said.

"What's over?" Nell asked, although she was pretty sure she knew. She set her broom aside and sat against the clapboards.

"Rose Cottage," Aunt Jerry said. She put her phone into her pocket and explained. It hadn't been a face-to-face meeting over coffee. It wasn't a video chat or a phone call, or even an official letter on nice paper. No, the Cozy Corners Sisterhood of Inns, LLC, had shut down Rose Cottage for good in a copied-and-pasted email. Nobody had even signed it.

Lulu slid out from under her wide yellow car. Its front wheels were up on little metal ramps and oil dripped into a pan underneath. She wiped her hands on a dirty towel and got to her feet. "That was fast."

Aunt Jerry shrugged. "Maybe it was a long time coming." She closed her eyes and raised her nose to the sky. Sunlight glinted off her sparkly glasses. "What a beautiful day."

"What happens now?" Nell asked. "Will they sell Rose Cottage?"

"Yes. From the way Ms. Tipton was talking, I think she's had all her ducks in a row to sell Rose

Cottage for a while now. It shouldn't take long," Aunt Jerry said. "You know," she added wistfully, "I always imagined myself staying here forever." She ran her hands along the porch railing. "Ow! Splinter."

Lulu put her hands on her hips and looked up. "What if *you* bought Rose Cottage, Aunt Jerry? Nell and I could help fix it up again. We're stuck here for the rest of the summer anyway. Why not pass the time with major home renovation?"

Aunt Jerry laughed. Lulu was being funny, but Nell could tell she was also being serious, too.

"Besides," Lulu said, "Nell still needs more human socialization before she's ready to interact with the general public at the Cape Green Companion Animal Shelter. Hanging out for a month with just you and me ain't going to cut it."

Nell opened her mouth to complain but realized her sister was kind of right. Lulu had managed to criticize Nell and defend her in the same sentence. That was one of the annoying things she was good at.

"I wish I could," Aunt Jerry said. "I really do. Rose Cottage is my favorite place in the whole world." She sat down on the front steps. "But I could never afford it."

"Probably some big company will come along and just turn it into another Peachy Skies," Nell said.

Lulu crossed her arms. "That's not a very nice thing to say."

"She's right," Aunt Jerry said, pulling a splinter out of her finger. "Anyway, I don't think I'm cut out for the cozy inn business anymore. I can't seem to keep up."

Nell spoke up—really spoke up, which surprised her even as she was doing it. "That's not true," she said. "There's a big difference between an artificial corporate bungalow with plastic plants, recorded birdsong, and rules up the wazoo and a *real* cozy inn. A real cozy inn needs the perfect innkeeper. And that's you."

Aunt Jerry beamed. She looked as though she were about to laugh and cry at the same time. "Oh, girls." She started to sniffle. "Anyway," she said, wiping her eyes on her flower-print sleeve, "At least you both will have time for your jobs and projects once you get home to Cape Green."

"What do you mean?" Nell asked.

Aunt Jerry wove her fingers together. "Once the Sisterhood sells Rose Cottage, I don't know where I'm going to live. There might not be room for you." She sighed. "I called your parents. They're expecting you home tomorrow."

The Netherbeast came bounding over, some kind of small creature's foot sticking out of his mouth. He jumped into Nell's lap and made a big *gulp!* The foot disappeared. Nell gave the cat scritchies on that magical spot where his jaw met his cheek and he chirped, "Mra! Mra!" with great approval.

"There's got to be *something* we can do," Nell said. Going home tomorrow! What about the Netherbeast? Her head was spinning. "What if we sold all the furniture?"

"It doesn't belong to me," Aunt Jerry said. "Everything in the house belongs to the Cozy Corners Sisterhood. None of it is worth much, anyway. Just Victorian clutter."

Nell didn't know what Victorian clutter was, but the way Aunt Jerry said it made her sad. Aunt Jerry *loved* Rose Cottage. How could she just give up on it?

It's a defense mechanism. The words suddenly popped into Nell's brain. Mom had said that to Nell about Lulu, one day when Lulu was particularly mean and Nell was particularly miserable. Nell hadn't understood at the time, but she thought maybe she understood now. Aunt Jerry was giving up in order to defend herself from the disappointment.

Nell looked up to the sound of a car pulling into the driveway. "Mr. Denver!" she said. "He'll have a solution!"

But it wasn't Mr. Denver's white van. It was a small, red car, and out of it stepped a squarish woman in jeans and a sweatshirt with cardinals on it, carrying a messenger bag.

"Mrs. Fennel!" Aunt Jerry clutched her collar. "The building inspector. She must finally have that report done."

Mrs. Fennel strode up to the porch. She pulled a single piece of bright yellow paper from her bag.

"That's not many pages for a report," Nell said.

"It's not a report," Lulu murmured.

"I'm sorry, everyone," Mrs. Fennel said, pulling out a stapler. She went up to the pretty, pink front door of Rose Cottage and stapled the paper to it. Then she turned to Aunt Jerry and patted her arm. "Jerry, I hope we'll still see you at Friends of the Library. Please give me a call if there's anything I can do."

Everyone turned to the paper on the door. It said:

Town of Deer Valley
Inspections Department
This Property is Hereby
CONDEMNED
AND UNFIT FOR
HABITATION

WELCOME

"What does that mean?" Nell asked.

Aunt Jerry shrugged sadly. "It means that Rose Cottage is beyond hope." She seemed to crumple inside her flowered dress.

On cue, Ms. Tipton's car sped up the driveway and crunched to a halt. She flung open the door and stormed up the porch steps. "This is *unacceptable!*" she roared, ripping the bright yellow paper off the door. "I came as soon as I heard. Where is that Fennel? How *dare* she condemn us!"

"I'm right here," Mrs. Fennel said. "And I didn't make this house unfit to live in. I'm just doing my job."

"Ms. Tipton, you've said all along that Rose Cottage is a disaster," Aunt Jerry said. "Isn't this what you wanted?"

Ms. Tipton spun around. "What I wanted? What I *wanted?*" Her eyes were practically popping out of her head. She waved the bright yellow paper in Aunt Jerry's face. "A condemned house is worth *nothing.* It will *cost* us money to tear it down! It's a *liability!* There's no *way* the Cozy Corners Sisterhood of Inns, LLC, can sell this place now. This is a *disaster!*" Her voice became suddenly quiet. "My own job could even be in jeopardy!"

"Welcome to the club," Lulu muttered.

"So what can we do?" Nell asked.

Ms. Tipton glared. "What the three of you can do is to get off Sisterhood property immediately! I don't want to see any of you here ever again."

VLOOP! The Netherbeast barfed up a hairball as big as a cantaloupe. It went rolling down the porch steps and squished to a halt in the grass.

Ms. Tipton pointed. "And take that disgusting cat with you!"

Aunt Jerry blinked. For a moment she seemed frozen. Then she looked down. Nell followed her gaze. The Netherbeast was winding around Aunt Jerry's legs, purring. His fur rippled with purple sparks the same color as Aunt Jerry's hair. *He's telling you to be brave,* Nell thought. But brave how? What did the Netherbeast mean?

Aunt Jerry looked up again. She straightened her spine. "I would like to buy Rose Cottage."

Ms. Tipton made a snappy *ppbth* sound. "That's the most ridiculous thing I ever heard. Nonsense."

Aunt Jerry pushed her glittery glasses up her nose and cleared her throat. "It's true, Ms. Tipton. I love Rose Cottage. I can't stand the thought of leaving it."

"The house is a catastrophe," Ms. Tipton said. "You couldn't possibly afford to repair it. I know what the Sisterhood pays you to manage this place—you couldn't even afford to tear it down."

"Nevertheless," Aunt Jerry said, "I'd like to make an offer."

Nell looked up at the house, thinking back to the first day they came. It had been angry then. Mr. Eslick's tantrums filled its rooms and vibrated its windows. Now it looked sad. Pale red shingles fluttered down like autumn leaves. The walls sagged as though they were too tired to hold up the roof. Somehow, Nell thought, Rose Cottage knew it was beyond hope. It needed Aunt Jerry.

"I think it's a good idea," Nell said. Aunt Jerry smiled.

"Nell, are you bonkers?" Lulu said. "You heard what Ms. Tipton said—it's a liability. That means it's more trouble to *have* than to *not* have."

"I know what 'liability' means," Nell said. "It's like an albatross."

"It's worse than an albatross," Lulu said. "There's no way Aunt Jerry can afford to fix Rose Cottage, not in a million years."

"I don't care," Aunt Jerry said. "I want to stay. The house needs me."

"What kind of game are you playing?" Ms. Tipton snapped. "The house is ruined. The land is a postage stamp. And all the furniture together isn't even worth the expense of moving it out!"

"I love the furniture," Aunt Jerry said. "It's full of memories."

"Jerry, you're not even legally allowed to live in this house," Mrs. Fennel said. "Never mind running it as an inn!"

"Well, that sounds like a poor investment for the Sisterhood," Aunt Jerry said, giving Ms. Tipton a steely gaze. "It sounds like the person responsible would be in pretty big trouble."

Ms. Tipton paused. "What's your offer?" she asked warily.

"My offer," Aunt Jerry said, "is a dollar. To get you out of this unfortunate mess you're in."

"A *dollar!*" Ms. Tipton said.

"But where will you live, Aunt Jerry?" Lulu asked.

Aunt Jerry looked around the messy yard. "I'll set up in the screenhouse for now." She looked at Mrs. Fennel. "If that's all right."

Mrs. Fennel patted Aunt Jerry's shoulder. "It's awfully drafty. There's no kitchen, no plumbing. It won't do for long."

"I know," Aunt Jerry said. "I'll figure something out. Once Ms. Tipton agrees to sell."

Ms. Tipton squinted so suspiciously, her eyebrows practically touched her nostrils. Nell held her breath. Her heart was thumping, but it wasn't moose nerves. It was excitement. She knew in her bones that Rose Cottage needed Aunt Jerry as much as Aunt Jerry needed Rose Cottage. Even if things seemed like a disaster right now.

"You're obviously sleepwalking or something," Ms. Tipton said. "But I suppose I can't really refuse. You'd be doing me and the Sisterhood a favor by taking this mess off our hands." She opened her handbag and pulled out a stack of papers. "The realtor gave these back to me when she dropped the house." She glared at Mrs. Fennel. "After *you* submitted your report." She flipped through the papers. "Sign here."

"You're making a huge mistake!" Lulu cried. "It's not worth it!"

"Rose Cottage might be unfit for guests," Aunt Jerry said, "but it's just perfect for me." She took Ms. Tipton's pen. She found the dotted line.

"No funny business," Ms. Tipton snapped.

"No funny business," Aunt Jerry said, signing her name with a flourish. "In fact, I've never been more serious in my life."

The Netherbeast flopped onto his back. "Good kitty," Nell whispered.

✦ ✦ ✦

CHAPTER TWENTY-NINE
A SCRAPING UNDER THE BED

Mrs. Fennel could only give Nell, Lulu, and Aunt Jerry twenty-four hours to leave Rose Cottage. The next morning, Nell and Lulu packed in silence. Their shared room was even messier than their rooms at home, with all the destruction the ghost of Mr. Eslick had caused. Pictures had tumbled onto the floor, the curtains lay in heaps, and the walls were covered with tiny cracks like spiderwebs. Still, the morning sunlight through the window was warm and cheerful. Bucky and Mr. Denver were coming over for breakfast. They could hear Aunt Jerry singing downstairs. It was hard to believe Rose Cottage was beyond hope. It felt absolutely *full* of hope. Was Nell imagining it? Or was it the house itself?

Lulu wound cords and tucked them into the pockets of her backpack. Nell folded T-shirts and rolled pants. The Netherbeast kept getting into Nell's suitcase, disguising himself as a ball of socks or a worn paperback of *Bunnicula*. Nell didn't have the heart to tell him he'd have to go back to the alley behind the mini-mart when they got home. She didn't have the heart to admit it to herself.

Suddenly, a tiny sound got her attention. A little *scrape-scrape-scrape,* like a cat scratching at the floor. She looked around for the Netherbeast, but he was quietly hiding in her suitcase disguised as sparkly black earmuffs with eyeballs.

Scrape. Scrape. Scrape.

What was it?

It was coming from under the bed. Nell lifted up the bedskirt and peered into the shadows. There was something *moving* under there.

"Lulu," she whispered. "Come look at this."

"What now?" Lulu said in an annoyed voice. She knelt beside Nell and they squinted into the darkness. "Huh. What is that?" Lulu got up. "Let's move the bed."

They pulled the bed out from the wall, which disturbed the Netherbeast, who thumped to the floor. Suddenly, his ears swiveled forward. His tail twitched. His front end got low and his back end got wiggly. If he'd been a regular cat, Nell would have thought he detected a mouse.

But there was nothing underneath the bed except a small framed print of a cow in a field lying innocently on the floorboards.

"What was moving?" Nell asked. "Was it that picture?"

"Don't be ridiculous," Lulu said. "Pictures don't move on their own."

"They do when ghosts throw them around," Nell said.

Lulu squished her lips together in the way that she did when she didn't want to admit Nell was right about something. "But there aren't any ghosts here anymore," she said.

"Well, maybe—" Nell stopped talking when the little picture started to *move*. All on its own. *Scrape, scrape, scrape.* It inched across the floor. Nell and Lulu stared at it with their mouths open. The Netherbeast darted forward and batted the picture off course a few times, but it always corrected itself and started moving forward again.

When the picture reached the wall, it started to climb. Directly above it was a nail. The wallpaper was discolored around the nail in a square patch that seemed exactly the same size and shape as the frame.

"I think . . ." Nell said. "I think it's going back to its nail."

Lulu made a gurgling sound. They watched as the picture climbed and climbed, slowly but steadily, up the wall, until it reached the nail. Then it settled into place and hung quietly.

"Holy cupcakes," Lulu murmured.

Nell reached for the picture.

"What are you doing?" Lulu said. "Don't touch it!"

But Nell had already taken the picture off the wall. She turned it over in her hands and ran her thumb along the wooden frame. Then she hung it back up. "It's fine now," she said. "It's just a regular picture of a cow."

Lulu crossed her arms. "Okay, so, that is definitely *not* a regular picture of a cow."

"No, really!" Nell said. "Look at my cat." Now that the picture was no longer moving, the Netherbeast wasn't interested. He sat giving himself a bath behind the ears. "He goes bonkers when there's something creepy going on. Uh, cats are like that."

"Look!" Lulu said. Nell gasped. All over the room, pictures and knickknacks were creeping back to their spots. The cracks in the walls were slowly sealing back up. Even the curtains were rippling ever so slightly, making their ways back to their rods at a snail's pace. The process was so slow and quiet, Nell wouldn't even have noticed if it weren't for the first picture's tiny scraping sound.

"So what does this mean?" Lulu asked. She reached out a tentative finger and touched the picture of the cow.

Nell puzzled it over. "I think," she said, "it means that all the stuff Mr. Eslick's ghost did wasn't exactly *right*, somehow. A ghost shouldn't be messing around with things in the real world." She grinned. "I think Rose Cottage is putting itself back together again."

The Netherbeast had noticed it, too. He padded from one corner of the room to the other, sniffing and listening. Finally, he sat dead center and peered at Nell with yellow marble eyes. "Mrow!"

"He's trying to tell us something," Nell said.

"Sure." Lulu tilted her head dubiously. "What is it, boy? Did little Timmy fall in the well?"

"No, really," Nell said as the cat continued to stare. "Will you just trust me? I know my own cat."

"He's not your cat," Lulu said, which was just about the meanest thing she could have said. But Nell ignored her.

"Meow!" yowled the Netherbeast.

"What is it?" Nell asked. She knelt down. "What are you saying?"

"MOW MOW MOW!" the Netherbeast crowed. Then he leaped onto Nell's nightstand, and from there to the open window. Nell raced across the room and looked out.

"He's sitting on your car," she said.

"He'd better not be!" Lulu stuck her head out the window. "Hey!"

Nell stared at the black cat, who was now threatening to apply his broken-glass claws to Lulu's pristine paint job. "I think he wants us to drive somewhere," she said. "He's a cat with a mission!"

"He's a mobster," Lulu muttered. But, to Nell's surprise, she unzipped her backpack and grabbed her keys.

CHAPTER THIRTY

THE CAT OF MY DREAMS

"Is there anywhere in particular your *cat* would like me to drive?"

Lulu was not convinced this was a good idea, Nell could tell. She had put on her gigantic sunglasses and was sitting with her hands tapping the steering wheel and a frown on her face.

But she was here. She had started the engine. Maybe it was something about Rose Cottage, or the Netherbeast, or Nell. Maybe the Summer of Weird Things was starting to rub off on her.

"I don't know," Nell said. The Netherbeast was perched in her lap, pawing at the glove compartment. With a pop, it swung open, and a glossy paper fell out. "Here!" Nell held up the paper so Lulu could see. "It's the brochure Ms. Tipton gave us!"

Lulu snorted. "Peachy Skies Cottage? Are you serious?" She put a hand to her forehead dramatically. "Wouldn't you rather not have to see Ms. Tipton again ever in your life?"

"Yeah," Nell said, "but my cat is pretty sure about this."

Lulu rolled her eyes. "Your cat is pretty sure."

"Yeah."

The Netherbeast headbutted Lulu's elbow and purred.

"Don't play nice with me," Lulu said. Then she sighed. "Fine. Whatever. It's not like this is the weirdest thing I've done this week."

Peachy Skies Cottage was only a fifteen-minute drive from Rose Cottage. Lulu's long yellow car bounced along bumpy back roads and sailed through the sleepy downtown.

They pulled into the driveway, and Nell got her first look at the Cozy Corners Sisterhood of Inns, LLC's new pride and joy. It seemed nice enough. The grass was shockingly green. There was no peeling paint, no saggy porch railings. The windows had tiny diamond-shaped panes like something out of a fairy tale. Nell knew diamond-paned windows were approved by the Sisterhood manual. Ms. Tipton had never liked Rose Cottage's big, plain windows, even though they let in a lot of sunshine and had great views of the garden.

There were three SUVs parked in the driveway, all extra large and extra glossy. "The Florentines!" Lulu said. Nell could tell her sister was a bit starstruck.

Inside, they found Ms. Tipton behind the front desk. The Peachy Skies guestbook was made of embossed leather and there wasn't a single puppy on it. Ms. Tipton frowned as Nell and Lulu approached. "If you think I'm letting you book a room, you've got another thing coming."

"That's not very hospitable," Lulu said. "I hope the Florentines don't hear you giving visitors that kind of attitude."

"What do you want?" Ms. Tipton asked. Her tone wasn't any nicer, but she spoke a little more quietly.

Lulu looked at Nell. Nell froze.

"Rrrow," the Netherbeast said.

Ms. Tipton practically jumped over the desk. "What is that revolting *cat* doing here? Are you trying to ruin Peachy Skies's reputation?" She squeezed her eyes closed. "Get out!"

With a tinkling of tiny chimes, a side door opened, letting in a summer breeze tinged with some kind of artificial floral scent that reminded Nell of the public bathrooms at Cape Green Beach. Fake birdsongs and cheesy music drifted through from the garden.

"*What* a glorious day!" a perky voice chirped. Two people in gauzy garments whooshed in from outside, practically knocking over Nell and Lulu.

"Oh, my gosh!" Lulu squeaked in a way that Nell knew her sister's friends would not have found cool at all. "You're the Flying Florentines! I can't believe it!"

"Lambchop!" the woman said. She was wearing sunglasses even more gigantic than Lulu's and a floppy hat that could have shaded a picnic table. "Aren't you delightful!" She held out a hand and Lulu took it in awe. Nell could hear all the woman's rings clicking together at the handshake.

"Locals!" the man said, looking from Lulu to Nell. He wore the same giant sunglasses and oversized hat. "Can you recommend any photogenic boutiques? Or scenic parks without goose poop? It takes our people *so long* to pick up goose poop. There's always so much of it. And the park rangers are *never* helpful."

"Never," the woman said.

"I'm not sure if the parks have goose poop in them or not," Nell said. She realized the words hadn't come out as moose honks and felt a bit proud.

Behind the Florentines, a stream of other people shuffled in from the garden. They carried cameras, coolers, beach bags, and makeup cases.

"These girls were just leaving," Ms. Tipton said, giving Nell and Lulu a look. She pulled a white cardboard box from the desk. "I have the croissants you requested. One low-niacin organic charcoal and one chia seed with extra gluten and sprinkled with edible glitter."

"Wonderful!" The woman opened the box eagerly. "I think this darling foyer will be perfect, don't you?"

"Yes, perfect!" the man said. They stood in front of a colorful plastic flower arrangement and each of them held up a croissant and smiled. Instantly, the team of people buzzed around them, holding up lights, swooshing fans, and *click-click-clicking* several tiny cameras.

The woman peered into the viewer of one of the cameras. "Perfect!" she said, and the Florentines threw their uneaten croissants into the trash.

"They're not going to eat those?" Nell whispered to Lulu.

"Ugh, you don't understand *anything* about travel influencers," Lulu said in a snooty voice. But Nell saw her sister look longingly at the delicious baked goods in the trash can. They were late to breakfast, after all. Bucky and his dad were probably already at Rose Cottage, and everyone was probably wondering why Nell and Lulu had run off. Nell was starting to wonder that herself, to be honest.

Suddenly, the chatter of influencers and the rustling of beach bags was interrupted by the most heinous noises Nell had ever heard.

"*MeeeeYOWW!   RrOWwOOOO! VReeeFFFFT! WaaaAAAAA! AAAAAA!*"

Everyone froze. Jaws dropped in horror.

"Your *cat!*" Lulu hissed.

Nell gulped. It was unmistakable. The Netherbeast had somehow commandeered the PA system and was now treating everybody to his terrifying arias at full volume.

"WHAT is THAT?" the Florentines gasped, holding their hands tightly over their ears. Their assistants rushed to place more hands over the Florentines' sensitive ears.

Ms. Tipton knew what was up. She looked daggers at Nell and Lulu. "Someone has brought their pet here illegally," she said, "but I'll take care of it at once!" She rushed out the side door into the garden.

"Don't touch him!" Nell raced after her. "He'll murder you! And eat your fingers!"

Everyone ran out into the garden. After a moment, the howling stopped. Ms. Tipton stepped out from behind a perfectly square hedge.

She was holding the Netherbeast by the scruff of the neck.

"How . . ." Nell started. "Scruffies *works* on him? Just like with other cats?" The Netherbeast's yellow eyes were filled with rage, but his bones looked like they were filled with Jell-O. *Good to know*, Nell thought.

"This is the culprit," Ms. Tipton said to the Florentines. "He and his irresponsible owners are leaving *now*, before I call the police." She dropped the Netherbeast, who somersaulted forward and came to a stop sitting up at the Florentines' feet.

"Fine, we're going," Lulu said. "Come on, Nell. Get your terrible cat."

"Wait!" two voices cried. The Florentines looked at each other. They seemed to be having an unspoken conversation. Their giant hats bobbed in unison.

The woman crouched down and peered at the Netherbeast. "This is definitely her," she whispered.

"Definitely," whispered the man.

Ms. Tipton looked suspiciously at Nell and Lulu, but they just shrugged.

Nell took a step forward. "What do you mean?" she asked the Florentines.

The woman stood up. "This cat—she's the cat of my dreams!"

"*He* is not for sale," Nell said.

"Yes, he is," Lulu said. "Fifty cents."

"No, no, no, you don't understand," the man said. "She *dreamed* of this cat!"

"She came to me in a vision!" the woman said. "She has a *message* for me! I'm sure of it!" She knelt down again and stared into the Netherbeast's gleaming eyes. "What is it, astral friend? What wisdom do you bring from the hidden planes of existence? What do you *want?*"

"A-*hem*," the Netherbeast said, and trotted off in the direction of the Florentines' large rental cars.

"We must follow!" cried the man. The Florentines hurried off in pursuit of the Netherbeast, their gauzy garments flowing behind them. Their entourage followed, struggling with all their gear.

"Hey!" Ms. Tipton barked. "Where does your cat think he's going with my guests?"

Nell thought about it. "He's probably bringing them home. To Rose Cottage." She wasn't sure why she thought that, but it felt right.

"He can't do that!" Ms. Tipton sputtered.

"Come on, Lulu," Nell said. "If we take the back way, we can beat them."

"Let's go," Lulu said, jogging to the yellow car. "Just when I thought today couldn't get any weirder."

✦ ✦ ✦

CHAPTER THIRTY-ONE
THE SWAN

"**W**hat are we going to tell Aunt Jerry?" Lulu asked as they sped into Rose Cottage's driveway and skidded to a halt next to Mr. Denver's van. She and Nell hopped out of the car.

"About the Florentines coming any minute?" Nell asked. "Or about *this?*" She pointed up at the house. Lulu gasped.

It wasn't the same Rose Cottage as yesterday.

If you squinted at it from a mountaintop in the distance, so far away that the house was just a tiny blob, you might be fooled into thinking it hadn't changed. The shape was the same. The color was similar. The size was spot on.

But everything else had transformed. The shingles Mr. Denver had worked so hard to install gleamed cozily like maple leaves. The clear glass in the large windows shone, framed by clean lace curtains. The sturdy front porch was like a welcoming smile. And all around, real birds sang and butterflies investigated the well-tended gardens.

"Girls!" Aunt Jerry rushed out the door toward Nell and Lulu. "It's *astonishing!*" Her smile was as wide as the porch. Bucky and Mr. Denver were right behind her.

"The house has *healed!*" Aunt Jerry cried. "We're back in business!" She clasped her hands together and twirled, her flowered dress flaring. "I can't wait to show Mrs. Fennel! Why, we can probably reopen *tomorrow!* And we'll do things *my* way. No more PA system! Puppies on everything!"

"Wow," Lulu said. "This house definitely isn't an albatross anymore."

"It's a swan!" Nell said.

"I don't know what happened," Mr. Denver said. He seemed dazed. "We came for pancakes and . . ."

"The house got better!" Bucky ran down the steps. "Nell!" He lowered his voice to a whisper. "Was it the Netherbeast?"

". . . I don't think so," Nell said. "I'm not sure. He's definitely up to something. But I think the house just . . . feels better. Feels right. You know?"

"Yeah," Bucky said, grinning. "Good job, Team Netherbeast." He stuck out his hand.

Nell shook it. "Team Netherbeast!"

"I know there are pancakes, but you guys have to listen!" Lulu said. "The Florentines are on their way here *right now!*"

"What?" Aunt Jerry stopped twirling.

At that moment, three fancy SUVs pulled into the driveway. Out hopped the Florentines, their assistants, and the Netherbeast.

"Is that your cat?" Mr. Denver asked.

The Florentines swished over to the sign, which looked as though it had just been painted. "Rose Cottage Bed and Breakfast!" the man read. "Isn't this where we were supposed to stay?"

"I think you're right!" the woman said. "That concierge at the airport said plans had changed." She put a hand to her floppy hat and looked up at the house through her giant sunglasses. "It doesn't look so bad to me. What do you think?"

"I think it looks rather quaint," the main said. "And that woman's purple hair is perfectly delightful."

"The Flying Florentines!" Aunt Jerry fluttered down the steps. "You're very welcome here! We were so disappointed you couldn't come."

"We almost didn't," the woman said, shaking Aunt Jerry's hand with a clinking of rings. "That marvelous cat from another dimension led us here."

Everyone looked at the Netherbeast, who was sitting on the porch railing. He seemed slightly startled. "Meow," he said, looking more like a regular, non-interdimensional cat than he ever had.

"Er, yes." Aunt Jerry gave the Netherbeast a wide-eyed look. "Would you like some pancakes?"

The Florentines looked at each other. For a long moment, neither of them spoke. Nell worried that Aunt Jerry had offended them.

Finally, the man said, "We haven't had pancakes in *ages*."

The woman laughed. "Why not? Should we? We should." She waved at the assistants. "We don't need you. Come back in an hour." Then she turned to the man. "Let's have a real breakfast."

CHAPTER THIRTY-TWO

ASTRARIA, WHO SPEAKS FOR
THE HIDDEN REALMS

*O*nce *you got to know them, the Florentines weren't that bad,* Nell thought. They were nice, actually. They answered all Lulu's questions, complimented Mr. Denver's father's pancake recipe, and made Aunt Jerry smile with all the kind things they said about her beloved B&B. They even took off their huge hats and sunglasses and ate their breakfast like regular people who didn't have to worry about influencing anybody.

But their favorite thing about Rose Cottage was the Netherbeast. "She's very special," the woman whispered to Nell.

"I know," Nell said.

After breakfast, the Flying Florentines said goodbye. "This is the most fun we've had in years," the woman said.

"Rose Cottage is the cat's pajamas," the man said. "It's the coziest, specialest little place we've seen in ages! We'll be sure to add it to our review of Deer Valley."

"Oh!" Aunt Jerry cried. "Thank you!"

Nell and Lulu exchanged a look. Would Rose Cottage get its five stars after all?

But then the man said, "I think we can give you three stars!"

The woman nodded, smiling. "How lucky!"

Aunt Jerry blinked. "Oh. Three stars?"

The woman laughed. "Oh, of course we'd love to give you five!"

"I'd give you ten!" the man chimed in.

"Yes," the woman said, "but three is our limit for Deer Valley. You see, we gave out five stars to a place in Trout Lake last week, so we don't want to repeat ourselves."

"Yes, so three stars it is," the man said, tapping his phone. "Annnnnnd—done!"

"Thanks again for the pancakes!" the woman said. "Check us out online! Don't forget to 'heart' and 'follow!'" And they hopped into their rental car and drove off, followed by their entourage.

Everybody watched them go.

"That was . . . weird," said Bucky.

"You don't know anything about travel influencers," Lulu said sadly.

Bucky crossed his arms. "I don't think I want to."

As everyone went inside to clean up, the Netherbeast hopped onto Nell's shoulders and went limp. His back legs oozed all the way down to her left elbow and his front legs oozed down to her right elbow. "What was all that about?" she asked him quietly. She steered away from the porch and flopped down next to a rosebush.

The Netherbeast rolled off her shoulders into the green grass, where he lay on his back, batting his paws at tiny flying bugs. "Roww?" he chirped.

"I mean, what was the deal with bringing the Flying Florentines here?" Nell said. "We helped the ghost. Rose Cottage healed itself. Aunt Jerry's going to be okay. Lulu can keep her summer job. Everything worked out. We didn't need the Florentines."

"Mow." The Netherbeast hopped into Nell's lap and started to purr.

"I guess they could have helped . . . well, *me,*" Nell said. "Is that what you were thinking? A five-star review might have changed Shana's mind?" She scritched between the cat's ears. "It's okay, buddy. I think Shana's right. People are a little scary sometimes. I don't always know what to say. I think I do need more practice. But don't worry—I'm getting better. I even made a friend—a human one! I'm sure I'll be a Junior Volunteer soon."

The sun made paisley patterns on Rose Cottage's lush grass and colorful flowerbeds. Even the concrete goat seemed a little taller and brighter.

Nell sighed. "What I really wanted was for you to be able to stay," she said. "It would have made Lulu leaving for college a little less sad. Don't tell her I said that."

"Mew," the Netherbeast assured her.

"Besides, we're a team. Teams shouldn't be broken up." Nell leaned back. The Netherbeast rolled off her lap. "But I guess we did our best. I can always visit you in the alley." She tried to say it with a chipper voice. After all, things weren't so bad. Almost everything had worked out for the best— Nell knew that in her brain. But despite that, inside, in her bones, everything seemed gray and dismal.

Nell's phone buzzed in her pocket. She frowned. "It's Barb." Tap. "Hello?"

"Nell! We just saw the Florentines' review of Rose Cottage!"

"Yeah." Nell rested her head on the grass in the shadow of the rosebush. "They work pretty fast."

Mom hopped on the call. "They said some very nice things about the B&B."

"It's a nice place," Nell said. "Aunt Jerry has been good to it."

"They also mentioned a cat," Mom said.

Nell's blood ran cold. She sat up. "Oh?"

"Yes," Mom said. "A cat belonging to one of the girls who helps out. Tell the truth, Nell—have you taken a cat in?"

Nell swallowed. She looked at the Netherbeast, who was now snoring so loudly he was alarming the chipmunks. *No,* she wanted to say. *I haven't adopted a cat.* It wouldn't be a lie. The Netherbeast *wasn't* a cat. Not really. And at the beginning of the summer, that might have been what she would have said. She might have been too afraid to speak up and tell the truth.

"Yeah," she said, heart beating a mile a minute. "That was me. I found him in an alley behind the mini-mart."

There was a long silence on the other end of the line. Nell thought she heard snatches of a fast-paced, muffled conversation.

"A cat is a big responsibility," Mom said.

Nell blinked. What did that mean? "I know," she said. "I take care of them at the shelter."

"They have stinky litter boxes," Mom said.

"Right," Nell said. If only Mom knew just how stinky the Netherbeast could be.

There was another brief silence, then Barb jumped on. "The Florentines are calling her Astraria, Who Speaks for the Hidden Realms. She already has over thirteen thousand hearts. She's a celebrity!"

Nell was stunned. A celebrity? The *Netherbeast?* "Uh," she said, "well, he's actually a male. I think. At the moment. But I thought you didn't like cats."

"Oh, Nell!" Mom said. "We love cats! Where do you think you get it from? We just know a pet can be a lot to handle for a young person."

"However," Barb said, "under the circumstances . . ."

"The circumstances being that Barb is obsessed with the Florentines," Mom muttered.

"Anyway," Barb said pointedly. "We think you're ready. When you come home from Deer Valley, you may bring Astraria with you."

Nell gasped. She laughed. She felt like rocketing up into the sky. "Really?"

"Really," Mom said. "I'm sure you'll take good care of her."

Nell looked at the Netherbeast lying in the summer grass, as squishy as a pancake, tail

twitching as he watched a monarch butterfly investigate a rose above him. "We don't have to say goodbye," she whispered. "Did you know this would happen?"

But the Netherbeast said nothing. He only blinked and swiped a lazy paw into the air, startling the butterfly.

Nell smiled. There were so many adventures in their future.

Acknowledgments

Thank you all the way to the dark realms and back to Ash Szymanik for bringing this story to life with their wonderful illustrations. Thank you to my scene-fixing mom, my hieroglyph-expert dad, and K, who always knows what the cats are thinking. Thank you to my terrific writer friends, including funny-rat advocate Katie Bayerl. Thank you, of course, to Joan Paquette and Hannah Dussold for believing in the Netherbeast. And thank you to Tiffany, Cindy, and the whole team at AMP.

About the Author

Adi Rule is an award-winning author of books for young people, including *Why Would I Lie?*, *Hearts of Ice*, *The Hidden Twin*, and *Strange Sweet Song*. She loves singing, breakfast, and video games. Adi lives in New Hampshire with a magician, a clowder of cats, a macaw, and a small but mighty flock of chickens.